SOMETHING DIFFERENT FOR CHRISTMAS

Sweet To Steamy Holiday Romance

DANYELLE SCROGGINS

PUBLISHING
WWW.DANYELLESCROGGINS.COM
Email: drdsellsmoreash!shing@gmail.com

CONTENTS

Published by: Divinely Sown Publishing

SOMETHING DIFFERENT FOR CHRISTMAS

SWEET TO STEAMY HOLIDAY ROMANCE

Copyright © 2019 by Danyelle Scroggins

SWEET TO STEAMY HOLIDAY ROMANCE

First Edition paperback

10 9 8 7 6 5 4 3 2 1

Printed in the United States of America

Book Cover Design by DanjaTales

Exclusive discounts are available for quantity purchases. For details, contact the publisher at the address above.

Printed in the United States of America

Dedicated to

To All My Sisters who are still singing "What Do The Lonely Do At Christmas?" Keep believing and in the meantime and between time, we read books as we wait on God to send the perfect man for us to love at Christmas. And, we also listen to the music we love. ~Danyelle

Here's Something for you...
The Something Different For Christmas Play List!

"Glory to God in the highest heaven and on earth peace to those on whom his favor rests."

Luke 2:14

I'm as successful, as Lady O if you asked my mother.

But lately, successful, saved, and satisfied is equaling stale, sarcastic, and stagnate.

I'm teaching young, gifted adults to become intellectually creditable, all the while wondering what has intellect gotten me? A nice house, car, and an empty bed that I refuse to allow anyone I know to lay in. I've outgrown satisfaction by self-sabotaging acts of sins and if another man ever gets close enough for me to take the bed, it's going to be after the night he and I wed.

So for now, I'm about to ditch my life.

New York City and my best friend is calling my name.

Food, fun, and my bff and the turn up is about to be real.

Nonetheless, I never anticipated Pierce Jansen.

He an intellectual, billionaire, and he loves the chocolate skin I'm in. Pierce also wants to do things to my body I'm not willing to let go down. All I wanted for Christmas was food, fun, fellowship, and a good vacation.

This tenacious, handsome, wealthy, older gentleman is

trying to turn my vacation into a blissful stay-cation. But did I mention, he's caucasian, wants to be married now, and for me, this is definitely *Something Different For Christmas.*

CHAPTER 1

This day is filled with so much excitement. Not much went on in my life other than the normal, but holiday cheer is definitely felt. I looked around my room, admiring the creative, vibrant, and stoic pupils. From the poised to the privileged and those poisoned by college campus freedom, all types of young adults grace my space. But to me, they are all future doctors, nurses, lawyers, politicians, and leaders for tomorrow, which is why I have given them the name, Scholars.

I take them and my job as serious matter because I do not need God chastising me for messing up the minds of a generation. See, once you move from the high school level, you are not so concerned with mad parents or angry grandparents keeping you from reprimanding or mistreating their babies.

These are now adults.

A part of being in college is to teach them how to handle their own business. But I cannot tell you how many times I've played parent. Told them what to do with professors who begin to believe they are God and mistreat them.

A story for a later date.

While others opted to cancel classes on the last day before the Christmas break, I decided on an early class to give each student a gift. Young college adults never expect anything from their professors, which is why I go out of my way to do something special for them. Believe me, my gifts are not gifts of pleasure. I specifically chose gifts to eliminate some of the stress of their parents.

Not long ago, I was the one making calls home for essentials like toilet paper, soap, towels, body lotions, and other hygiene needs. I could have used my extra money to purchase what I needed, but that didn't happen. The need, desire, and aspirations to not only party but be slamming at the party—dressed to impress from head to toe—canceled any thought of me buying anything worth having.

Not only does my gift bless them, but it blesses their parents too. I simply bought a square basket for each student and filled it with the things they would never purchase for themselves. Hand sized lotions, soaps, and scented sprays for both genders from Bath and Body Works are my signature items.

The news of my Christmas digs spread the campus like wild-fire. Every year, my classes get larger and larger, thanks in part to the Christmas baskets.

I turn my attention back to the fifty-four young adults talking amongst themselves.

"Well, scholars, I'm delighted that we've come to the half-way mark of our semester. Your projects have been graded, and if I must say so, you guys rocked."

The young adults roared with cheer.

They deserved this celebration because my mid-year project entails the bulk of their grade. If you didn't do well on the project, you'd be seeing another college philosophy professor or me—if required for your major—again.

"I appreciate the thought you put into the project. I'm sure some of you are destined to become some powerful speakers and great thinkers. Always be mindful of the notions you pick up and the prejudices you embrace. John Locke said, 'There is frequently more to be learned from the unexpected questions of a child than the discourses of men, who talk in a road, according to the notions they have borrowed and the prejudices of their education.'"

Some of the students recited the quote with me. I laugh.

Them reciting with me is a pure testament that they're listening and repetition works. But behind the smile I'm sharing is complete sadness. All I can think about is me teaching The Scholars to become intellectually credible while I'm swimming in my intellectual pool of loneliness.

I shift my mind away from my emotions and continue my little speech, "I pray for you all to have a safe holiday, and on your way out, grab a basket—guys on the left and ladies on the right. Be blessed, Scholars, and remember to find questions to ask instead of pretending like you know the answers. Merry Christmas, Happy Hanukkah, Feliz Navidad, and to those who do not celebrate happy break."

The young adults laughed, and some shouted, "Thank you, Professor Prince."

After the last student left, I gathered my belongings and triumphantly walked the halls. My red-bottom heels hitting the floor like a strutting thoroughbred who won the race. As much as I loved my scholars, I love a much-needed break.

Professor Gordon must have heard my heels because there he is, sticking his head out the door. I swung these size sixteen hips a little harder in my fitted black dress. He's probably now staring at my bump. It's too little to be called a butt, but perfect enough for my height to be considered a bump. It works for me, and I'm not tempted to add anything to it but a cute skirt, pair of jeans, and a girdle to make sure it's steady and never wobbles.

Moving quick, I don't look twice at him because there's not a married man in this land that can do anything for me. Sure, they may oppose; their lust problem is not mine. I'm waiting patiently on my Boaz. Not a broke, cheating, or fake-az but Boaz. Like the one who found Ruth.

Someone planted in this earth rim to cover me, and although I still haven't run into the brother yet, I wait. The reason you'll never catch me slipping, I want to be found.

When I leave my house, I'm purposely trying to show a brother what will be on their arm. I'm bothered by women who say they want husbands, but they dress like a hit and run. Not that it's any of my business, but you attract based upon what you look like.

I told the women in women's life class you'll be single forever if you look like a holy maid. We are saved. We don't have to look like we belong on the compound, riding a buggy, and with a bonnet on our heads.

I tell my scholars, you can't expect a man to notice you for anything other than sex when you are at the store in your bedclothes. It's you throwing out signals, then getting mad when they approach you for sex. Practice how to dress to impress.

I'm practicing while I wait. My momma doesn't go to bed with a scarf on. Nor does she forget her perfume or some sort of scented spray. And to my knowledge, she's always worn cute gowns and good clean panties.

Her theory is, if the ambulance ever has to do a pickup, she'll be smelling good, with clean panties on, and no unattended holes on her body. And, believe me, I learned from the best. You will never find me slipping, and if you do, I'm in the place where looking raggedy is expected—a hospital.

Looking decent is not my dilemma. The dilemma I'm having is knowing how to step out of my circle. I stay in the same cycle expecting something different, and it isn't happening. So, this Christmas, I'm doing something different.

Quanie is pushing me out of the cycle-circle that plagues my life. My rut. And even if I'm not ready, with tickets already purchased, I may as well be prepared.

Momma and Daddy are a little perturbed, but they'll be fine. They've been holding one another down for thirty-seven years, and I haven't had a boyfriend since I left college. So in the words of my students, this year, I'm saying, 'Deuces Baby.'

I'm getting out of here, and I've made sure that I'm not returning until two days before my break is over—all I need.

Two days to fall back into my rut.

CHAPTER 2

The December wind is blowing in Louisiana with temperatures ranging in the low sixties, which is the only reason I'm second-guessing Quanie's choice. In Louisiana, our winters are not winters at all. If we happen upon some snow, we better have our cameras ready. It only sticks around long enough to build what I consider a counterfeit snowman, throw a couple of ice balls, and it's over.

Daddy did buy me a mink coat like Moms, and I've never worn the darn thing. You pull out a mink in Louisiana, you'll look like a complete fool trying to prove you rich. But in New York, it'll be fine unless it starts to snow and the coat gets wet.

Of all the places in the world, Quanie and I could be going to for Christmas—her want-to-be-a-snow-bunny-self—wants us freezing in New York City. Who does New York in December? No one other than someone who's watched too many *Sex In The City* reruns but never saw the episodes where it got ten below zero. But here I go, following my little sister into only God knows what to keep her from doing only God knows what.

Yep, I said little sister because she was my only hope. As

holy as my parents are, they failed the multiplying part. I'm their only child but thank God for huge favors. I went to college and met my sister, the one mom did not give birth to, Quanesha Rachelle Montgomery, but to me, Quanie.

As a dorm hall monitor, I met all incoming freshmen. Quanie was one of them. The girl was smart, witty, and nothing short of amazing. But yet a dare-angel who pulled me into dares I knew were illegal for a saint. In college, I played the role of saved because if I were filled, God would have chased me back to Louisiana.

I came from a holistic background, and when I got to college, I ditched the long skirts and socks for a pair of Girbaud jeans and a tight t-shirt. Thanks to Quanie. Clothes my Daddy would've preached an extra thirty minutes on top of his already two-hour message against.

Quanie, let's say her grandma had her in the same lane, but she knew how to sneak around getting freedoms I could only imagine. The girl was wise beyond her age, and she helped me come out and find Daiya. Those were the days. I'd go back if I could, and the only thing I'd do differently is never going home.

I love Louisiana as much as I love my coffee, but I hate being everything to everyone, and I don't know who I am.

But as usual, Quanie and I are still running to each other when we're going through something. For months, she's been a little bit too hushed, hushed for me. I can feel it in my belly. She's been hiding something. But I still had to respect the fact she's a grown woman and give her the chance to come to me and the space to do her.

I'm still not sure about all the ends and outs of Quanie's situation, and of course, I have questions, but they can wait until New York. Her drunken ramble and this pressing desire to go to New York to spread some cookie-cheer are ridiculous. But again, I knew something was going on. And honestly, I'm praising God for the effects of wine. It will make the quietest people tell all of their business.

I'm definitely not judging because I, for one, am grateful Jesus turned water into wine. Sometimes, a virgin daiquiri is my only mode of relaxation. Daddy and I fell out about drinking. I reminded him of First Timothy, the fifth chapter, and verse twenty-three, which reads, "No longer drink water exclusively, but use a little wine for the sake of your stomach and your frequent ailments."

It is the Bible, and I'm sticking to it.

Like she needs me, I need her.

Quanie's faithful pull or kick in the butt reminds me, I am not my parents or my job. Coming from someone who knows you almost as much as you know yourself is trusted. She doesn't know the Bible but is quick to say, 'The Lord didn't want you to be saved and live in a stupor. He came so you may have life more abundant and live free indeed.' That part.

But I came back from college, got a safe job, took on another full-time position as youth director at my father's church, completing my circle: work, church, home, a weekly ritual. The only thing new in my world is the brand new clothes hanging in my closet looking at me because I'm too scared someone will ridicule me if I wore them. Sometimes, I want to walk away from all the isms, but not God.

I sort of wish I could believe in God, do the things I enjoy doing, and not have to worry about who's running back to my parents with *ish*. But the folks in my town are still tattling on a thirty-year-old woman like I'm thirteen. It's the life of a P. K.— preacher's kid. The reason why I even considered freezing.

I'll take frostbite to my butt rather than spend another Christmas driving my parents as they make rounds to all of their members' houses. Not happening. I know Daddy was disappointed, but my body clock is moving. Does He not understand I refuse to be like his friend Bishop Hall's daughter?

At thirty-nine, she married a man she didn't love, nor even liked. All because she was approaching forty and the thought of not having a baby overclouded her judgment. She swindled the first duck she could find, and they didn't even stay together a good year. But the reality is, she got what she wanted, a baby.

It couldn't be me. Daddy could roll over four times in his bed or grave before I marry to have a baby. Science is too far advanced. I'd be like the main character on the sitcom, *Jane the Virgin,* having a baby by myself.

It is probably what my Daddy is afraid of, but I remind Mother to keep her husband out of his daughter's business before I go ham. A college professor said, "Go ham?" Yes, because going ham is much more dignified than saying, "Make me cuss him out."

Trust me, I know how far to go. I respect my Dad's anointing. I don't like old school authority, a dictator-ish spirits knowing how to make my pressure boil. I'm as sweet as a lamb, but if you push me, I'll come out fighting like a street alley raccoon.

Guess who I get it from. My Daddy. It's bad enough I'm here doing everything they want me to do, except marrying Jeremy Holmes, my Dad's second assistant. He's got some sugar in his tank I don't care to taste if you asked me. Every time I tell Daddy about it, he can't believe Jeremy could be swinging from men to women and preaching.

Down low or low down, I've seen it all on the college campus and in the pulpit. So, no thanks, Daddy. When I have sex, I want it to be with someone who knows he's the giver and not pretending to be the receiver.

Say what you feel. I'm thirty. Not dirty.

These are the realities in my world, and what trips me out more than anything is all the old saved folks who pretend they

SOMETHING DIFFERENT FOR CHRISTMAS

don't know. Then, be like my parents, sitting at the kitchen table trying to figure out if it's the devil or one of his imps.

I can't blame everything on the devil because he has to have a body to perform in. And unlike some of these evangelical Christians, I'm concerned about more than abortions and making slaves of people who have as many rights as them to be free.

Who's even considering folks need to be freed from sins? I can't toot a horn for the sins I hate, then close my eyes to the evils resembling my own. To God, sin is sin. I tell my Daddy to call it all out because fornication and abortions aren't the only sins. The love of money and lying is as bad.

CHAPTER 3

It has been five months and twenty-seven days since I buried my wife. The stillness of days and nights' quietness sometimes makes me want to take a pillow and blanket and lay on top of her grave. But what would it help? She's resting in the bosom of Abraham, and I'd be sleeping amongst the sobering spirits of grief held captive in the graveyard.

I know she's in a better place, but it doesn't mean I'm not jealous. I would have gladly traded places with her. Although she begged me to let her go, it still doesn't make this easy or stop me from asking, "Why did you have to leave me?"

Kate and I were married in our senior year of college at the University of Texas, and we couldn't wait to move to New York. Neither of us had ever experienced winter, but we made it beyond the shock of our first winter experience, and we were still doing it until the day she died.

But I took my Kate back to Texas because our family lives there. Her parents and mine have outlived my Kate, but God has an untraceable plan which must always be trusted.

Now, here I am, a forty-six-year-old bachelor, widowed, no

children, and successful. But I'm as lonely as the taxi drivers who can't wait to get a patron to talk to.

I might miss her, but I'd never want her to endure the pain of cancer as she did again. Kate was as tough as a wisdom tooth. She survived it three times before the fourth and final stage of aggressive lupus returned. And I replay her last words in my head.

"Pierce, I love you, and I've loved you since the day we met. Don't die when I die. And don't forget to live. Now you are free to get you a woman with the melanin skin you love so well. And I'll be rooting you on and praying you don't tell her your lame jokes." We both laughed, and an hour later, she was gone.

Always our little inside joke since the first time I laid my eyes on Viola Davis. I gasped. Not because I didn't like Blacks or African Americans, but because it was like staring at a goddess. There is something so special and smooth about the skin of a black woman, intriguing me as much as it entices me. And who better to tell about my fetish than my wife. My best friend.

Kate made life so fun. Most men wouldn't dare tell their wives what they honestly think, but not me. I could tell her anything. She listened and often told me exactly how she felt.

But even as she spoke to me, it wasn't time to look towards my future. Not when my past slipped away beyond my control, as I with adamant intentions, tried to hold on. I'd spent millions flying her all over the world in search of a cure, and yet, nothing.

Kate got tired of it all; including the flights, doctors, treatments, needles, and prayers not answered as we hoped. She and I both agreed and understood death was the answer. We reckoned death to be her transition from sickness to wholeness. The ultimate decision of a sovereign God to free Kate from the troubles of this world.

Even now, I don't cry when I think of her. She's living in

blissful happiness while I'm stuck here, still having to guard my heart and mind against the evil one who is plotting to kill, steal, or destroy. Kate would be so blessed.

I'm grateful. God gave me the time He did with a woman who fulfilled me in ways only she could.

Although I can never replace Kate, one day, I surely would love someone in my life who has the type of faith and fight as Kate.

We built companies, houses, and bank accounts together. And all because Kate trusted God enough to have faith and to make Him our first investment partner.

I'd be the first to admit, it took me some time to get with the tithing thing. Kate was eager to tithe. All it took was for her to hear someone say, 'making an investment to God is like standing on a stock exchange platform and never coming down.'

We did, and I'm still up.

Now, I have to see where the Lord is going to take me.

Standing in my 7 AV office window, peering down at Times Square, which seems to be as busy as usual, I can't help but smile. Kate always told me as diverse as the people who walked the streets below our building, so would be my family. I never understood what she meant, but Kate was the type of person who said the Lord showed her stuff, and you believed it because what she said came true.

She saw the future, and all I could see was loneliness. I sort of embraced the feeling before she even died. I was trying to mentally prepare myself for what was coming, but I promise I failed. Now, it's time for me to start doing something.

I rarely do anything anymore besides show up here at my office, but this week, I'm making a vow to go out. It's my first Christmas holiday as a widow. Really not the word I'd like to describe me as, but I could never call myself a single man— concealing her memory.

Clubbing? But before the thought could register well, I say to myself, "I'm too old for drinks in the club environment."

A forty-six-year-old man club hopping is still searching for, running from, or trying to run up on something. Either way, the hunt can lead to destruction, and I'm way too old for foolishness. I'm convinced you get whatever the environment you're in is presenting you. And I'm only accepting what will uplift me, not tear me down.

Instead of take-out, I'm going to hit some notable restaurants and remember Kate as she were, instead of as she became. But I'll start this weekend. Maybe a lounge.

CHAPTER 4

My luggage lay on my bed like the clothes would jump off the racks and land perfectly folded. I laugh at myself because I have enough coins in the bank to pay a maid to do my chores. But what's the use? Then I'd definitely become my parent's maid.

I plopped down on my bed and pulled a pillow on top of my head. Torn between my thoughts and dilemma, I closed my eyes. The conversation between Quanie and I floated through my mind.

I laughed first, thinking this drunk nut called me asking could she send a letter to Santa Claus.

"Daiya, you are turning into an old woman who's doing everything for everyone except yourself. Let's go somewhere for Christmas. Let's do something neither of us has ever done."

"What the heck are we going to do, Quanie? I won't take another girl's trip to New Orleans. So what else is there to do?"

"Let's go to New York. We could stay until Christmas."

"Quanie, do you know how cold it gets in New York? My body isn't used to cold weather."

"That old stale body isn't used to anything, but churching, teaching, and care-taking."

We both burst out laughing.

No matter how sad it is, it's been my life ever since I moved back home. No one around me sees I'm drowning. To think, I'm supposed to be skilled at untying mental knots and analyzing complicated situations, but I'm finding it only works when you're on the outside looking in.

I teach, smile, talk, church, pray and do it all in mode functioning while broken. But everyone's too busy getting something from me, and they can't notice the one fetching stuff, supplying, and fixing them, is broken herself. The tears cascading down the sides of my eyes are a pure indication that if I didn't go on this trip, I'm about to explode.

Whether Daddy knows it or not, this is the Lord's doing because this sister was heading towards double jeopardy. Touching God's anointed and dishonoring my parents, and all in the same sentence.

What's amazing? I allowed myself to get this deep in the ditch of my oppressions. How many times have I said in speeches, caregivers need care? Too many. Even I ask myself, who's the caregiver? Then I answer. You are you dummy. And, the two over seventy parents you care for are your patients.

My point is that a grocery store experience with my mom is like taking a child to Wally World for the first time. She sees and wants everything but needs nothing. So I spend half of the time pulling her towards what we came for and the other half fighting long lines with four cashiers but thirteen lanes closed.

The walk to the car is as complicated as the shopping experience. But for my Mother, I always have time. I trust my expertise, which instructs me to stock everything she needs before she's out, minimizing our grocery shopping trips.

I remedied those long mall hauls by teaching. Mom is such a quick learner. I taught her how to spend her husband's money shopping right in her favorite recliner, and she does it well. I often forget Momma earned a degree from a prestigious HBCU but chose to raise me and be a wife to my dad as he requested, required, and expected.

To be honest, she's definitely the reason why I've stuck around. I'd hate to leave her to handle Daddy all by herself. Now, if Dad makes her mad enough, she'll drop her First Lady title in a minute. And all you hear him saying is, "Now, now, Alma. God wouldn't be pleased with how you are speaking to me."

I snicker every time at how quick he is to put God in it after he's stirred up the mess. My Dad reminds me of a child who digs in an anthill with a stick and screams bloody murder when those ants attack him.

I'm done crying and trying to allow my mind to talk me out of this trip with this parental consciousness. It's about to be on and popping, and I'm doing what I want without feeling guilty.

Everyone calls me an old soul; sweet way of calling me an old maid—the reason why pastor's daughters struggle to have a boo or get married. I know a lot of pastor's daughters still single.

They bop around their father's ministries hated by the women and avoided by the men. One half doesn't want to offend the preacher with the thought of having sex with his daughter. And the other half wants a freak and thinks she's too holy to be the mother of his children. The guy I liked told me, "I couldn't make love to you the way I desire for feeling like I'm doing something you are too holy to do."

What? I almost choked on my spit, thinking, are you serious? But I could tell by his eyes he was. Then my mind started wondering what he wanted to do, and I cautioned myself to stay in my lane, stay holy, and wait on God.

Cause nine times out of ten, if you have thoughts of doing it to me, you've already experienced it with someone else. And don't get me wrong, I'm not saying I need a virgin or someone who's never experienced sex. I need someone who hasn't been spreading himself from city to city and house to house.

Is that too much to ask?

Maybe, God will eventually answer my prayers, but until He does, I'm going to enjoy traveling to the places I can afford and changing what I can change.

And furthermore, I'm sick and tired of singing the song *What Do The Lonely Do For Christmas?* Every year I'm singing the music, and I've never taken the time to answer the question. So here it is, the lonely put on their cute clothes, go to the family gathering, look at all their married cousins who cheat, and they thank the Lord, it's not them.

So for all the folks who think they have themselves something, and looking down their noses at the lonely, be careful. Laughing could be detrimental to your relationship.

Each year, I deal with being single, and I binge out on books and Hallmark movies. And although I'll be in New York, I think I'll add in a few Lifetime movies. These stations are competing against one another by showing more women of color who look like me.

Believe me, I still have hope.

I will not lose my hope. God will one day send me a man who loves me unconditionally. What I'm not going to do, is jump in pot with boiling water hot enough to scold me.

I'm not getting burnt by a man who only wants a good time and runs around town pretending to be Santa Claus. He's checking his list, doing it twice, trying to find a girl who'll be naughty for one night.

Not me. I still have hope.

I'm willing to be Santa's Baby if he's willing to show me there are still some good men in the world who are searching and praying as hard as me for love.

Think of it as Santa meets Cinderella.

I don't have the step-parent mess. I come with a pair of loving parents who love God and the church, a best friend who cusses like a sailor, and a job requiring me to share knowledge, devotion, and love wrapped in concern.

If he can handle my baggage, then I can take anything he brings to the table.

Daiya, get out your head. You still need a bad outfit.

CHAPTER 5

Every day leaving the office was becoming harder. Not because I didn't love our home. I dreaded the thought of being there alone. My secretary suggested I get a penthouse apartment. At first, I thought it to be wasteful and crazy, but I succumbed.

I purchased a three-bedroom penthouse, with a home office, huge dining room, beautiful kitchen, and a living room overlooking the beautiful skylines of New York. For what I paid for it, I could have purchased twelve ranch style homes in Texas.

Watching Kate leave the earth unable to take her half or even a penny of the money we've made changed me. I'm spending our money on whatever makes me happy, including: supporting the charities we love, buying my wants, making sure my sister and Kate's brothers' children are getting the best Christmas gifts ever and giving healthy bonuses to my employees. All the things I love.

I gave my secretary my black card, and she furnished the place in all white, my favorite color. I had not one complaint. I only wished I would have moved Kate to this place before she died. Maybe the change of scenery would have given her hope. *Wishing thinking.*

Kate loved everything about our fantastic lake-view property on Skaneateles Lake. I came home from work one day, and she informed me of our move. It was right before her second battle with cancer. If anyone asked me, I'd say the house was indeed an incentive to live.

She fought.

She was able to live another four years in the home she'd created for us.

I still love the place, but sometimes, it's such a reminder. All the good days, filled with laughter, the food, friends, and family, especially on the holidays, now hurt. Meanwhile, everyone is too busy feeling sorry for me to even come my way.

It's crazy how death causes the masses to swarm on you like the beehive. Cooking, cleaning, laughing, sharing memories, and before my Kate could even get in the grave good, everything stopped.

The everyday calls, spontaneous meals, emails of concern, and even the occasional texts all stopped. Don't get me wrong, there were times when I wanted to stand in the middle of my living room and yell, "Get the heck out."

I cautioned myself, unlike Jesus, who threw everyone out of Jairus' house but Jairus, his wife, and His disciples. I knew as quickly as they came, they'd forget. All the laughter turned into a dead silence, I alone handled without holding grudges. I'd rather the quietness of days than the cheers of those who claim how hard it will be to live without Kate, but none of them actually knows.

The night attendant greets me and opens the door to my limo. Butch Hobbs is his name, and he's a good guy. I've had the privilege of meeting his family and even playing a game or two of dominos with him.

"Good evening, Mr. Jansen."

"How are you, Mr. Hobbs?" I greet him in the same manner by which he greets me. He says, "Yes, Sir," and I do the same towards him. Why? Because money has never made me think I'm more than Mr. Hobbs or any other black man who lives and breathes the same air God gives me.

And I realized the first year after I married Kate, she was the one who had the power to get wealth all over her life, not me. I would still be working in a corporate job, hating it with every passing day, and sucking up to my boss had she not had enough faith for her and me.

My family has the type of home they have because we bought it. My parents would still live on their one-acre country lot, but God saw fit to change their circumstances when He changed mine. Kate's parents, a little more well-to-do, took some time to accept me with their daughter. Figured she could do better than me, but Kate knew me.

I want to tell black men most white people aren't prejudiced towards blacks. They're discriminatory towards the broke or lacking. They care more about the color of your bank cards than your skin and making sure you aren't opening a wallet with an EBT card publicized.

Money, the power to get wealth, and an excellent portfolio have the potential to change your skin color.

"I'm good, Mr. Jansen. How about those Cowboys? Were you able to watch it?"

"Mr. Hobbs, I tried, but I promised it ran my blood pressure straight up. We're on the fourth string quarterback, and he almost won a game. If he had a little run game, we might have pulled it off."

"Mr. Jansen, I said the same thing. Man, I was about to lose my mind. I apologize."

"For what?"

"I called you, man."

"Heck, Hobbs, I am a man. If you would have done like my wife used to do in one of our gossip sessions and called me, girl. Then, I'd have a problem."

"She did it too. So does Martha—too much."

"It's universal." They both laughed.

"Well, enjoy your night, and if you need me, ring the phone."

"Thank you, Hobbs," I shook his hand and slip him an envelope as he punched the button to my floor. "Have a good night, my brother, and tell the wife, Merry Christmas."

"You too, Mr. Jansen, and thank you. She'll go to shouting when I give her this." Hobbs waves as the elevator closed.

I laugh. Little did he know, I'd give any amount of money to hear Kate call me girl again. *He who finds a wife finds a good thing and obtains favor with the Lord.*

CHAPTER 6

S miling hard, I walk through my favorite department store, waving at two of my students, who are clerks—a few others who knew me by name speaks. I would be ashamed if I weren't First Lady Alma Prince's daughter. My Mother has pull—as my students say—in the city, but I call it shopping divs.

Mother could shop the average woman into a stupor, but me, I've learned from the best. My only problem is fear. The fear of wearing something my students may associate me with one of them, or something causing my father to disassociate me as his, blinds me.

I planned to be incognito—wearing a long skirt and shades —but it didn't work. Like my Momma's, these broad shoulders and the curly puff taking over the top of my head make it hard to go unnoticed.

Two sales ladies approach me.

I already know what's on their minds.

"I use *Curl Enhancing Smoothie* by Shea Moisture," I said, and they both laughed until one spoke.

"How did you know what we were going to ask?"

"I noticed you both were natural, and anytime I'm approached by natural ladies, I know what they need. Enjoy the product ladies," I walk by them as though I've done my good deed for the day. And they call out, "Thank you," but I shake my head, turn back and smile, and keep it moving.

Finally, I make it to the evening-wear department. I cringe. Too many dresses to choose from, and the specific instructions not to get anything my mother would like, keeps ringing in my head. I carefully and precisely find seven different dresses to try on. Knowing full well, each dress would cause my Mother to have a hissy fit if she saw me in them.

After allowing the clerk to give me a tag, I vanished into the last stall. The dressing room is large enough for me to feel at home and in the cut enough to allow me to hide. I place my purse on the bench, take off everything except my half bra and body shaper, and pull out my iPad. "Siri call Quanie."

"Calling Quanie." I giggle.

"Quanie," I screamed like a maniac when her face appears on my screen. "I'm in the dressing room and ready, and I followed instructions well. I got all the dresses with the potential to make Daddy preach longer, and Momma shout. "

"Good, that's exactly what you needed. Now come on, put the dress on, and let me see."

"Okay, I'm starting with this champagne dress. I think it's my favorite."

I slipped on take it off. The front has a V stretching from the breasts to my stomach. These busts are too huge for this.

"Turn around and let me see the back."

"Really, Quanie."

"Yeah, really, now shake a little and stop complaining. I'm helping your drive."

I shake my butt.

"Girl, stop shaking like you're seventy and shake like your thirty."

"Quanie, ain't nobody gonna twerk at a Christmas party."

"How do you know? After a man sees you in that dress, you're liable to be doing anything."

I roll my eyes, "Quanie, you not me. And stop all the hoochie dancing over there."

"See, that's why you need to leave Louisiana and get a man because ain't nobody saying hoochie no more."

"I'm still saying, 'hoochie, hoochie.'"

"Girl, put on the next dress."

I tune all of her shenanigans out and put on the black dress. It's sort of like a long A-line dress, but the back drapes and falls down right above my bump. I like this one. "Quanie, what about this one? I like it, but."

"But what? That dress looks good on you. And I know what you're thinking. It's too much skin showing, but you have to get out of your comfort zone. And at the end of the day, if you don't like it, return it."

"After I've worn it, Quanie?"

"How much is the dress, Daiya?"

"It's two-fifty."

"Hell yeah, return it. If you don't, I will. But in all seriousness, that dress was made for you, and you'll see it's not as bad as you think it is."

"Okay, so I'm going to get the black one."

"Now put on the other one because I've got to go."

I put on the red dress with one sleeve out, and I feel like Cinderella. The bottom hugs me in all the right places, and the mermaid tail is off the chain. But still, there's a sense of nervousness creeping in because I'm not used to sexy dresses.

"Daiya, get out your darn head, and I only used darn for the sake of respecting your wishes. That dress is fire, and if a man doesn't want to put you in his car and take you home after wearing that dress, he's dumb and stupid."

"But you do know I'm not riding or going anywhere with a stranger, right?"

"Girl, get off my phone."

"Bye, I chose the black and red dress?"

"Daiya, stop acting brand new and get those dresses and get out of that store. You need to hurry up and get here tomorrow."

"Okay, Mudea."

"You're the one always acting like a mudea. I'm so glad this old woman spirit is about to break off you."

"Now, you need to get off my phone. What you know about breaking spirits?"

"I might not be holy, holy, but I know a little something, something. Now, bye, I love you."

"I love you too," and Daiya ended the Zoom.

CHAPTER 7

"**D**aiya, put your sunglasses on, make these purchases, and head towards the door." I remind myself as my feet were moving quicker than a booster, walking fast to escape being caught. *Quanie and her foolery still makes me laugh.*

She snickered. "I'll be the bomb or crazy in these dresses."

On a bad day, I would have only bought one, but it was a good day. My tone abs were on point, and I didn't run into any of Dad's parishioners. It's a good day in the neighborhood. Even got out of the store before anyone except the clerk could see my haul.

Jovial and coo-coo is how I felt, and at the same time—all types of mixed emotions stirring within. I'm buying dresses adding no protection from the cold but fitting me like a glove. *Silly Daiya.*

One-stop left to make.

My thought is interrupted by the sound of Mother's ring-tone. I blow out a breath, hoping she's not telling me another thing Dad said about me leaving. I mashed the button on the steering wheel with hesitance and say, "Hello, Mom."

"Hey, Baby, are you stopping by? We know you leave tomorrow, right?"

"Yes, ma'am, you need something?"

"No, you've already made sure Dad, and I have everything we wanted and needed. Come on by, and drive safely."

"Yes, Ma'am," I answer her and hang up the phone.

Well, two stops.

Five minutes later, I turn into my first stop, *Ulta's* parking lot. This is makeup heaven for those who love enhancements, but it wasn't my thing. Someone put the memo out in the holiness church makeup meant whoremonger. So to keep the peace, I only wear lipgloss.

To wear or not to wear was the high topic in my youth Sunday School class. And being a Philosophy major, I always make the children argue or should I say, debate their prospects while at the same time answer each other's questions. For whether it's an ethical or moral instruction—I believe the old church's way was simply to teach what they showed in their own conduct.

So I answered my babies, I have worn and will wear makeup if I desire, but I can do without it when I'm in the presence of those who prefer me not. But Quanie couldn't care less about my isms. Although she was a shade lighter than me, she always ended up touching me up and mixing colors to fit my skin. This time, I'll surprise her. I'm buying a makeup bag and filling it with everything I need and don't.

Eyeliners, mascara, and then I work my way to some beautiful eyeshadows. I'm perplexed. Do I get one with glitter or not? The application clerk must realize I'm as lost as they come. She shows up to help, and I quickly put her to work.

"Please beat my face, and whatever you use, I'll buy it. But the catch is, you have to take it off too." The girl's eyes got huge. First, I use the word beat, which means to make it look so good if my face were beat, you couldn't tell. At least, I believe it is their theoretical meaning of the term. Second, she's about to make some coins. I hope she doesn't pile this stuff so thick, I'll have to buy the entire section.

I sit patiently as she implements her skills. Lady turns me around to the mirror, and I don't even know myself. I looked behind me to make sure Daiya hadn't died and left God's spirit in the chair as my twin. I take two selfies to make sure Quanie does it like this, then sit back so she can take it off.

I must say, I'm impressed. With everything from the magnetic eyelashes to the gold lipstick, it was all me.

I walked out of the store feeling accomplished, then it hit me, on to my parents. *Lord, please don't let Dad still be on this guilt trip. I'm too close to flying to have him in my head. And please, Jesus, help me to close my mouth.*

Ten minutes and I'm pulling in the driveway whispering, "In Jesus' name. Amen."

Pushing the bronze handle and the door simultaneously, I let myself in then I started yelling. "Mom and Dad, where are you?"

"In the kitchen," Mother yells back.

"Good evening, parents." I hug my Dad from behind as he sits at the head of the table.

"Hey, princess," he answers.

"Hello, sweetheart. Do you have everything ready for your trip?" Mom asks, stirring a pot of something smelling absolutely delicious.

"I do, Mom."

Dad shoots a furrowed eye in her direction, "Mother, why did you go there?"

"Because Prince," she calls him by our last name as a sign of respect, "whether you say it or not, the girl is going away for Christmas. Now, you better get used to it, or you'll be moping around this house like a pathetic nut."

"You always know what to say, Alma."

She shoots back, "It's the truth."

"Please, you two. I stopped by to hug you before I leave in the morning, not to start an argument. Now, Dad, stop being petty, and Mom, you're mean."

"Child, your Daddy needs to understand you're a grown woman. He'll be alright."

"And your Momma needs to learn when to talk and when not to talk."

Daiya shook her head because he wouldn't leave well enough alone. Her mother's mouth was moving ninety-miles-per-minute, and now he decides to be quiet. He wasn't right until she chopped on his neck, and now he's looking like a wounded puppy.

Daiya walked over towards the stove and patted her Mother's shoulder.

"Calm down, Mom. Stop letting Dad egg you on and look at him over there. Looking like his best friend told him off."

"He needs to stop, Daiya. He's going to keep on until he runs you clean off, and then what? You help me, and Momma appreciates you for it. And he's trying to run my help away. No darn well, some lazy women at the church who don't want to go to the store for even themselves. They sure wouldn't want to go for me."

"I understand, but we've let Dad say whatever he's wanted to say forever. And now, he's not satisfied until you almost cuss him out. I wonder what those good church mothers would think if they saw how he acted."

"Now, don't go trying to pull church folk in the family business, Daiya. I'm sorry, Alma."

"For what, Prince?"

"For running my mouth. Daiya, I'm happy you are doing something you've always wanted to do. I'm going to keep in mind you are a grown woman who has the right to live your life how God and you desire."

"Thank you, Prince," Alma said, coming over to hand him his plate and stand by her husband.

"Let us pray. Father, we thank you for our only child. We pray You would cover Daiya, the pilot, and the plane, and do the same for Quanie. We thank You in advance for Your traveling grace and arriving mercies. Now bless this food and hands skilled to prepare it, and let it be nourishment for our bodies. Clean any infirmities, and we declare the food and water You supply heals us, in Jesus' name. Amen."

"Amen," Daiya and Alma answered in agreement.

"Are you eating, baby?" Mom asks me, and I roll my eyes.

"Of course. I'm not letting Daddy eat all those smothered pork chops by himself. Not tonight, I won't." And they all laughed.

CHAPTER 8

Laying in my bed, I awaken, realizing I'm moments away from a trip with my bestie, but for Christmas. The jitters in my belly are beginning to feel like nauseous waves of anxiety, but right when I even think of canceling, my phone starts ringing. Quanie is calling.

"What's up, old spinster?" She asked as soon as I said, "Hello."

"Whatever, gal, I hope you are packed and ready?"

Knowing her, she's rolling her neck as she speaks. "Don't worry about me. It's you who I have to worry about pulling out. You know you'll change your mind in a heartbeat, and I ain't having that."

I'm joked out because there's no need to deny or lie. I simply say, "My mind is made. I need this as much as I need water." Convincing myself not going on this trip would be failing to give me the necessities of life.

"Good, so did you make sure to get warm clothes?"

"I did, and I'm bringing the mink coat I've never worn, and my bomber jacket. I also made sure to pack two sets of gloves, both with scarves, hats, and earmuffs. Sister will be warm."

"Good deal."

"And Mom got us both these feet warmers you drop in boots."

"She's such a doll, but her husband."

"Quanie, don't talk about my Daddy. He prayed for you last night and cracked Mother and me up."

"I can hear him now, "And that Quanie.""

"You know him don't you? Well, charge it to his head and not his heart. And I'm getting off this phone, so I can call for my Uber."

"Okay, safe travels, and I'll see you soon."

"I can't wait and the same to you. Bye."

I hung up the line.

"Siri to call Uber."

"Calling Uber."

After doing the math, it was cheaper for me to get a lift than to leave my car at the airport. Mom would have been happy to drive me, but Dad wanted to ride. I couldn't risk him purposely making me miss my flight.

He's been known to thwart my plans and then act as if it were God's plans all along.

I stuff down breakfast, grab my cup of Keto coffee, and head out the door. This coffee is giving me life and keeping me in these sixteens at the same time. Momma tells me I need to lose weight, but little does she know, these hips are honey and more precious than any piece of money. So, I pass. I'm making Keto coffee to keep all the extras pounds away.

My full-figured body is a blessing to me. At least, I'm finally embracing the whole me now. It took me to get to size sixteen before my bump became noticeable. Little does Mother know, a single man at church told me, "You're not a lady until you reach one-eighty," my spirit came all the way up. God stirred up the gifts and gave me peace surpassing all understanding.

I promised myself I would not buy another diet plan, eat

another Weight Watcher meal, nor would I pop another pill. I'd be happy the way I was and love the skin and body I'm in. If the Keto coffee keeps cutting my cravings and giving me energy, I'm good.

If a man chooses me, he has to take me as I am. The only thing I'm willing to change is my last name and bad habits. Everything else will be a part of the packaged deal.

I greet the Uber driver who gets out and opens the trunk for my bags. He smiles, and his dimple is as cute as his Arabian skin-tone.

"We're headed to Shreveport Regional, correct?"

"Yes, and can you please watch the bumps?"

The driver looked through the rearview mirror at me, "I will. It's a shame we're riding on these bad streets."

I nod my head because he was right, it is a shame, but because the mayor is young and black, I try not to say much because I don't like to dis my own. I simply reply, "It is, and although this administration has made a lot of street improvements, there's still room for more."

The driver doesn't feel the same. "There is, and if they stop arguing over simple stuff and get together to make a difference, maybe the city will see changes."

I nod again, but my mind quickly goes back to the Bible, "... *Every City or house divided against itself will not stand.*" The division is so prevalent until the side who wants the edge is quick to go to the news. But the things concerning the citizens, like unanswered murders and bad streets, are still undone. But again, I keep my opinion to myself.

We pull into the circle and in front of my departing airline. I'm happy we made it to my destination because I'm tired of talking to a stranger about the streets, and he's not paying any taxes in the city. As a matter of fact, he sends money to his family overseas and does not produce a dime in taxes in the U. S.

I'm for anyone who can work and pay taxes coming to the melting pot. I'm not down with me paying high taxes and them making ten times the amount I make—peddling hair products and food—and not paying one cent in taxes.

By the time he opens his trunk, I'm cold, as in hot mad. So cold, I wait on him to pick my bags up and put them beside me.

"Thank you," I gather my things and give him two dollars over the fare. My average Uber tip is ten dollars, but I'm not tipping anyone who's talking about my city. I'm paying for a billboard when I get back saying in bold black letters, *Only Tax-payers Have The Right To Talk Trash.* Period.

CHAPTER 9

Meetings, meetings, and more meetings. Sometimes this is the only thing bothering me about my businesses. Kate loved houses, I loved music, and she believed the world had a spot for us.

We bought tons of real estate, flipping houses to restore communities. The flips lead to us becoming contractors and renovators. Kate also became a broker and opened her own real estate and brokerage agency and a mortgage firm. She made me get licensed and first-hand schooled me in all things concerning commercial contracts, selling, and building. You'd be surprised at how many buildings Kate and I own. Heck, I'm now the sole owner, and it still surprises me.

I don't like sitting at the table with people who basically woke up intending to talk you down on your price as if you need their coins. I'm sitting here like I'm all in, but the only thing going to keep my mind on this meeting is an offer of one-hundred-twenty-million for my prime downtown spot their eyes are on.

It's next door to The Wellington Hotel, owned by one of my

good friends. To be honest, I'm making sure whoever buys the building will benefit him and me.

When I literally tapped my thumb on the table, my assistant knows this meeting is basically over. And because Brad knows me so well, he stands to address the room.

"Well, gentlemen, Mr. Jansen has another meeting in an hour, and since we've come to no agreement, why don't you reschedule with me after the holidays."

"The holidays?" the gentleman questioned Brad, and I know it is time for me to step in.

"Mr. Adego, you heard Brad correctly. After today, I'm on vacation, so if you want my property before the holidays, it's now or later."

Mr. Adego looks at me with piercing eyes, and I stare right into his. One thing you cannot do is scare me. Cancer took the scare right out of my heart, and after it, I make the daily declaration 'God hasn't given me a spirit of fear, but power, love, and a sound mind.'

"Jansen, we will give you until after the holidays to change your price. If not, we will find another property."

"Adego, you won't give me anything and by all means, search for another property. My price went up to two-hundred-million."

Adego huffed, but Brad had already called my bodyguards to escort Mr. Adego and his flunkies to their car. I smile and say, "Good day," as they are basically put out.

For years, I played the game like a dumb little college dude who needed the funds, and these people walked all over me. Now, I'm a full-grown forty-six-year-old man who doesn't have time for games. Either you in or you out. I've spent thirty years in a marriage teaching me daily tomorrow isn't promised. I don't have time to waste time, and all I have is right now.

And I'm for sure not wasting time on an arrogant prick

who thinks he's running something. I've watched investors like him play people out of their possessions and turn around and sell them for three times the amount they paid. Not on my watch.

I hit the buzzer on my intercom, and Brad answers.

"Renew each ad to reflect my new price and do not take any meetings, calls, or emails about this property until after the New Years'. And Brad, Mr. Adego, is not welcomed on this property until we have an official apology from him and his staff."

"Understood, boss," Brad answered.

"Thank you, now go enjoy your family for the holidays. As a matter of fact, tell everyone in the office it's time to go home. But make sure you give them their Christmas bonus."

Ever since our first Christmas in business, we've given our employees and a nice bonus. I usually allowed Kate to do whatever her heart desired, but this was my baby. I didn't want any of my employees struggling like my parents at this time of year.

For most parents, this is the time of year when money gets funny. But not if I can help it. The bonus started out as three thousand dollars. Now it's up to twelve thousand.

I'm in my office, but I can hear my employees telling Brad to thank me. They are happy, but I don't want them feeling sad for me. Today, I miss Kate more than ever. She'd have me dressed in a Santa Claus suit as she put on a Mrs. Claus outfit. We'd hand the employees their envelopes and hug each one.

Today, I don't have the strength to do it.

I'd hug them and fall out crying like I did at Kate's memorial. I had convinced myself I was all cried out. I was going to sit through her memorial, nodding at all the beautiful words about my Kate, smiling as the choir did renditions of old hymns, and hug all of her Sunday School babies who wanted a hug. Needless to say, it didn't go as planned.

As soon as I saw my Kate lying in a casket lifeless, it felt like someone stuck a dagger in my heart. I cried. I cried until I could only whimper, and then I think I went numb. Person after person pay homage to my beautiful, loving, and caring wife, but I didn't hear anything.

By the time we got to the graveyard, I was out of sorts. I begged Kate to allow me to put her in a mausoleum, but she refused. She kept reminding me the Bible said the grave will give up her dead, not the wall. And I did what she wanted me to do. I laid her to rest beside her grandmother and other relatives. I shake my head to come back to now.

I need a drink, and tonight I don't want to go home by myself. I'll eat at The Wellington. No, maybe, Keens. Nawl, The Wellington. At least there, I will feel like I'm amongst family.

CHAPTER 10

My plane ride was smooth and quick because a sister was blessed enough to find a flight with only one stop. For six-in-a-half-hours, I read two books and played a couple of games on my iPad. My bestie arrived in New York a couple of days before me, and I hope she hasn't done anything to make me ashamed.

It didn't take getting off the plane to feel the temperature change. By the time we passed the Carolinas, my knees had begun to ache, causing me to snuggle in my travel blanket. I'm praying the feet warmers, boots, and this fluffy white scarf does what they were created to do. I walk off the plane, through the sky bridge, and towards the JFK baggage claim area.

Once I get there, my attention is grabbed by a man holding a sign with my full name. I smile because Quanie knows I hate feeling lost, and she sent assurance. I'll ride and die for my girl. I walked up to the gentlemen who wore a warm and pleasant facial expression.

"Hello, I'm Daiya Treshelle Prince." I extend my hand to shake his hand.

"Hi, I'm Deacon. Ms. Q. Rachelle Montgomery sent me to pick you up. I'm the driver from The Wellington."

"Thank you. I need to get my bags."

"Point them out, and I'll get them for you."

"Awesome," I responded and wait patiently until my designer bags came around the conveyor belt. I pointed them out, he retrieved my bags, and I followed him to a black SUV. *My girl is already in New York showing out. I wonder whose arms she twisted to have the hotel SUV picking me up.*

By the time we make it to the hotel, I'm exhausted. I wouldn't dare drive a car in New York. I was in the back of the SUV, mashing the floor as if I had breaks. My legs and feet are tired. He yelled out an explicit, and I silently pray. *Lord arriving mercies is what I need.*

Who was happy to get to The Wellington Hotel was me. I thanked the Lord and blessed Him in Jesus' name, and as soon as I said, "Amen," my door opened. The driver uses his hand strength to steady me as I exited the SUV. Then he hands my bags to the connoisseur, and I give him a twenty-dollar tip. Ten dollars over my usual, but I was so happy to get to The Wellington Hotel. I had to give him more.

I walk through the grand doors and the opulence of the hotel—in an instance—captivates me.

"You are admiring this hotel like I'm admiring you."

I look towards the sound. I find a gentleman in a grey two-button Brioni suit behind the deep African accent staring at me. I'd know this brand anywhere because I've been shopping with my Mother for my Dad's suits since I was six-years-old. Mother always dressed Daniel Prince in the best.

"Hello," then I add to my greeting, "It's a pleasure to meet you. I'm Professor Daiya Prince." Making sure I publicized my credentials. I extend my right hand, and instead of shaking it, he brings it to his lips and kisses it.

"My name is Dareek Adego, and the pleasure is all mine."

I nod, smile, withdrew my hand from his, and then looked around, but didn't see Quanie. As Mr. Adego was about to ask me something, I heard screaming from my left, capturing both of our attention. I turned towards the sound, and I too started screaming.

It's Quanie. We scream, hug, and jump around like two girls who opened a Christmas gift box and found their favorite doll. We both forgot we weren't the only people in the room.

Quanie looks at me and then at the gentleman who was noticeably caught in the gander of our affection. I pull her into my embrace, "Girl, I'm so happy to see you," I said, holding on to Quanie as if I could squeeze away anything she was facing.

She lets me go, and the first thing she says is, "*Bish*, we in New York." I have to excuse Quanie, but at least she gives me the slang cuss word instead of the actual. "Daiya, I've been waiting on you all morning. How was your flight?"

"It was good, sis. This is Mr. Adego. I met him."

"Uhm, hum," Quanie is too happy about seeing me to even care.

I waved goodbye to Dareek and turned my attention back to Quanie. "I'm ready to get to this room so I can take a bath and eat. But anyway, how was your writing session going?"

"It's not. We'll talk about that later. Come on, let me ride up with you because I've already checked you in to your suite, and I have your keys."

"Exactly why I fool with you."

"Did you bring your dresses?"

"I did, and knowing you, plans to show it off is already made."

"You know me, we don't have to leave this hotel to get glamorous. All we need to do is dress to impress, and the place will come beckoning?"

"Girl, nothing has changed, has it?"

"A whole lot has but right now, all I want to do is focus on you getting in this room and enjoying this vacation. *Bish*, I hope you brought some cute fits cause you ain't rockin with me looking like no country saint."

"I already know, and trust me, I'm prepared to go out and shop for anything I need."

"My girl!" Quanie high-fives me and then opens the door to my suite. She hands me a key fob, and I stuck it into the side pocket of my purse.

"Okay, sissy, I'm going to go and give you a chance to relax. I'll call you in a couple of hours, and we can go grab a bite to eat."

"Sounds good to me." We hug one another again. "This is going to be an awesome trip. *And maybe this Rachelle person can get back to being Quanie.*"

I simply hug her and say, "I love you, sissy." She says it back and then leaves.

The room is as luxurious as the lobby. The chandelier is probably worth more than my vehicle, and the plush white furniture looks like clouds. I walk around the suite admiring the decor and the layout. Everything screams money and lots of it.

I open the french doors to the bedroom and grasp. This is the kind of room you get for a honeymoon, and here I am without the honey. I retraced my steps after hearing a knock on the door. Maybe Quanie is ready to tell me what's going on.

I open the door, and the bellhop asks if he could put the vase of flowers on the foyer table. I nod, eager to see who has sent me such a beautiful arrangement.

I motion to grab my purse to tip him, but he assures me the tip has already been given. I nod, smile, and follow behind him to lock the door. After I've secured the lock, I race towards the flowers to grab the card. I open the small card, and all it says is, *'I'm not leaving this town until I see your beautiful smile, Dareek. P.S. Would you have dinner with me tonight?'*

I blush because I'm thirty-years-old and I've never gotten flowers from a man before. I don't know if the shame's on the men around me or me. If he's sending me flowers and we just met, I'm doing something right.

I'm about to relax in this colossal tub and see if I can vision myself with the chocolate drop, Dareek.

I quickly rebuke my own flesh. I don't need Satan trying to entice me to commit any sins against myself. I specify and say aloud, "I need to see if he can be nice company. He is a chocolate drop, but he can't get none of my chocolate."

Now, I'm relaxed.

CHAPTER 11

The office is quiet, and the only person left is my bodyguard, Chuck, who Brad asked to stay, and I agreed. It's better to be safe than sorry, and these days, I choose safe.

Tonight, I'm going to eat at Carson's place. I can use some company, and he's always a good dose of laughter. And not to mention his love for Kate and me. I guess if I would have had a son, I'd want him to be like Carson Wellington.

I walk up to the hostess at the hotel's restaurant.

"Good evening Mr. Jansen."

"Hello, there."

"Your table is awaiting you, and your coffee was placed on the table as you walked up."

"I'm so thankful for how you girls take care of me."

"You're welcome," she says and escorts me to my table.

I already know I could take any of these girls home, but I refuse to play with children. Most of them haven't either figured out what they want to be in life or how to accomplish it. I smile but give her a hundred-dollar tip.

Her eyes glisten, and I realize the money is as much needed as it is appreciated.

"Robin, right?"

"Yes, sir, it's Robin."

"Why were you about to cry because of a tip?"

"I. You know Mr. Wellington doesn't like us sharing our personal business with the guest."

"Well, I've been coming here long enough to not be a guest anymore. If it helps, you can call me Uncle Pierce. Now, what's wrong."

"I have a five-year-old, who I had to tell Christmas won't be the same this year. With so much going on in the world, things have been slim, and people aren't tipping like they were."

"I understand. What's your address?"

"Mr. Pierce, I actually live with a friend."

"I'm not coming by for me, I'm sending your child something, and after tonight, I don't want you to worry anymore about his Christmas."

"Yes, sir, and thank you so very much. The address is twenty-one forty-four, Jackie O Lane."

"Thank you, and when you get home, everything will be done."

"Praise the Lord," she yelled and cried even more.

"Jansen, what have you done to my hostess?"

"Wellington, how are you?" He laughed. "I'm being Santa."

"I know you like a book. What are you eating tonight?"

"The ten-ounce sirloin with a stuffed baked potato and green beans."

"I'll take this to the chef, and how would you like your steak?"

"Medium well."

"You got it," Carson Wellington beckoned for a waiter and gave him the order. "May I?"

"Man, this is your fine establishment, and you can sit anywhere you desire."

"Thank you, but you are still our guest, and we respect your choice. How's the sale of the building coming next door?"

"I thought I had a buyer. A guy named Dareek Adego."

"He's a guest here for a couple more days. The guy is way too arrogant for my taste."

Pierce shook his head. "Mine too. He's the flashy type trying to prove a point—to everyone—he's a top-notch businessman. Might would be a good guy if he'd scale down a little."

"My sentiments exactly. He had some flowers sent to one of our other guests and tried to make my receptionist give him her room number. We don't operate like a two-star establishment."

I laughed then added, "He's tripping hard, and who does he think he is?"

"I don't know him from an ax murderer. I've never had a murder at The Wellington, and today won't be the first. He was hot, but what we ended up doing is allowing the gift shop clerk to give them to the connoisseur."

"Wise, and I increased the price because he was so out-of-line, and from the looks of things, I'm not comfortable with him being anywhere near people I consider as family."

"Boy, what a weight off my shoulders. I was wondering how the meeting would go. And, I think I could use the building as an extension or an overflow for this conference. What do you think about that?"

"I understand, and if you talk about the devil, he will show up won't he," Pierce nods at the hostess desk where Dareek was checking in for a table. "But that would be perfect since. It's yours."

"Well, enjoy your meal, and let me handle him to make sure he's not abusing any more of my employees."

I nod, "We will talk later."

Carson nods and scurried to the front of the room to help Robin seat, Mr. Adego.

I'm happy he didn't notice me, but if he had, if the young fellow disrespected me in any way, I'd be forced to put something on him. Folks like Adego won't do anything to incriminate themselves in public. I pulled my newspaper out of my bag and began skimming through the pages. Watching the news on television has never been my thing. I prefer to read the newspaper, while most Americans are reading blogs.

By the time I made it halfway through the paper, the waiter had approached my table with my food. I moved my phone to the other side of me and made space for the plates.

And in walks my future.

CHAPTER 12

After taking an hour nap, I'm starving. My stomach woke me up. It's used to eating five small meals a day, and today, I've failed. This morning, I enjoyed two slices of bacon, an over-easy egg, and my Keto coffee, which were long gone. I called Quanie's cell phone and room phone to ask if she was accompanying me to dinner, but there was no answer.

My mind wonders where in the heck she could be, but I'm talking about, Quanie.

I pull my clothes out of my bags and decide on my grey sweater dress, black leather knee boots, and my black leather jacket. Pulling my naturally curly hair out of the scrunchies, I shake my head, allowing the curls to fall.

The side part is always cute. I'm splitting, fluffing, and pulling at the same time to make sure it falls right, and you can see my hang-time.

Now, I'm ready. Big hair don't care.

I take my credit card out of my purse and slipped the hotel key in my jacket, admitting to myself I've never been in a hotel where the key fob looked like something for a car.

But everything is high tech these days.

Viewing myself in the gold-trimmed wall mirror, I winked and attributed myself as the co-creator of the beauty who stares back.

No panty lines, girdle dents, body shaper invisible, and bump sitting high. She's on point.

I leave my room, prancing down the hall and to the elevator, humming, *This Girl Is On Fire* by Alicia Keys. By the time I made it downstairs, I take a deep breath and follow the arrows leading to the dining restaurant. When I arrived at my destination, I surveyed the place, tilting my head around the hostess to see if I could see him.

"Good evening, ma'am. Table for one?"

"I'm meeting a gentleman here, Dareek Adego."

"Sure, let me escort you to his table."

Head high, passing all of the patrons who were either conversing or eating, I smile at an older gentleman who's staring as if he knew me. He doesn't look familiar at all, but I grin because he sort of reminds me of Burt Reynolds. In thoroughbred mode, I strutted right up to the table where Dareek sat. His eyes intensely focused on me as he disconnected a call, stood to greet me, and assisted me as I scooted into the booth.

"Thank you for the flowers," I said, and he smiles as if he'd hit the jackpot.

I wanted to say, "It's going to take more than flowers—to get me or my goodies—so stop smiling." But instead, I smiled back.

"Good evening, so you're a professor?"

Who starts a conversation with a good evening and a question? I see where this is going but play nice, "Yes, I am."

"What subject? If you don't mind me asking."

Maybe it was the way I looked at him, but he'd read my thoughts because you want to know too much too soon.

My eyes furrowed. I can feel them. 'Be nice,' I tell myself, "I educate in the field of Philosophy."

"Interesting."

"How so?"

"Well, I love reading, especially books by philosophers. When I was in college, I got a revelation from this quote, 'We are never present with…'"

And I joined him, "But always beyond ourselves; fear, desire, hope, still push us on toward the future, by Montaigne," I concluded. Looking him square in the eyes. I pucker my lips a little, thinking to myself, *It's the quote arrogant men rehearse to act as if they understand faith and chance.* I wish I could train my facial expressions to ignore bull, but it's hard.

"Wow, you are the first woman who's been able to recite with me. Where have you been all of my life?"

"Can't tell you because then, you'll know too much about me. So, do tell me about the quote."

"I realized as much as I felt comfortable in my space, there was always a nagging within pushing me. Whether it was fear, desire, or hope, everything I have ever done or not done has been by the enticement or these three things."

"I understand, but I believe without skepticism, there is a God who controls the universe. He has the power to endow you with passions, cause you to move beyond fear, and place a passionate desire on you to embrace the things you hoped for. This type of hope is produced by faith—and initiated by the belief God can do anything—except fail."

"Although I believe in hope, I do not believe in God as a Jew. Your ancestors have handed you down through generations a Jew, and I can never make a Jew my sovereignty."

"I was always taught God is a spirit, but the Son of God was born through a Jewish woman, giving Him the earthly identity of a Jew. But whether He was a Jew or considered by His own a phony full of heresy, I believe He was, is, and is soon to come."

"So you are a Jesus lover waiting on His return?"

"Call it what you want, but yes, I believe in Jesus, and He is the Christ. I also believe there is no way unto the Father except by Him. So though I can give an answer for this great hope I have, and can easily contend for the faith, I refuse to use presence time persuading someone who has undoubtedly answered his own questions."

"Don't get feisty. I'm not questioning your belief."

"You may not be questioning my belief, but you are questioning my God. And I'm too grown, tired, and smart to entertain religious foolishness."

"I don't believe it's foolishness. I thought philosophy was about asking questions and searching for the answers. But, you already discarded me like my questions don't matter."

"Goodnight, Mr. Adego. It's apparent to me your questions aren't questions. They're statements, and again I say, I'm too grown, tired, and smart for foolishness."

I scooted out of the booth so fast, I gave myself a rush. You uncircumcised Philistine, who are you to talk about my God. Not on my watch. I don't care how good you look in the Armani blazer, and silk black shirt opened enough for me to see your chest hair. I'm needy, but I'm not greedy, and I recognize the enemy and lust.

In thoroughbred mode again, I swing my hips, strutting hard and hoping he's getting an eye-full. I look back over my shoulder, and he's doing what I thought he'd be doing. Lusting after my bump. But knowing arrogance when I see it, I've made the hunter even more intent.

I slip in the Business Center door and watch if he's trying to follow me. He did and is. Standing looking around like a plumb nut looking for a ghost. Call me lady ghost. And who's in the ducked off hiding space, Quanie.

"Girl, what are you doing?"

"Ditching crazy."

"Where he at," She's looking over my shoulder, trying to see.

"Quanie, to think, my mouth is watering for a juicy steak, and he trips. I sideways want to fight."

"Calm down, mudea, he done ruffled your feathers."

"I showed him today, big girl, don't play. Let's go eat."

"Oh no, ma'am, what you won't do is have me go into that lounge looking like this, and you look like that. By the way, you're cute. Give me a second. I'll be back in a few."

CHAPTER 13

I keep looking over in the direction where she went. What beauty? Her chocolate skin and body remind me of the perfect Hershey bar, smooth with nuts in all the right places. I can't see her, but I have a feeling she's meeting Dareek Adego.

Taking more bites of my food, anxiousness is contributing to a feeling of being full. Then frustrations of why someone so beautiful would waste the time of day on someone so prideful sets in. *Do not covet thy neighbors' stuff.* I ask the Lord to forgive me. It's apparent, I'm jealous.

I finish eating my dinner, and not long after, she struts back past my table and out of the restaurant as she strutted in. This time an air of anger rested on her. *Was she his wife? But I didn't see a ring on his finger.* And moments later, I see him moving as if he's trying to catch her.

She's long gone as far as I can see. I'm delighted she realized an arrogant prick isn't worth her time. I see him standing in the foyer, looking every way, but by the expression on his face, he's pissed he can't find her.

I turned my attention back to my meal, and Carson appeared.

"Jansen, did you see what happened?"

"With what?"

"You know like I know. I saw your head and eyes." Carson laughs.

And I know he's peeped me out.

"The egomaniac must have run her off. She got out of here so quickly, and I watched it all from my office. I turned my cameras on, and now, he's standing in the hall looking for her."

"Where did she go?"

" She ducked off in the Business Center. "

"Are you serious?"

"She must've known he would come after her."

"I'm sure she did."

"Is she still in there?"

"Yes, and he looked like he gave up. When I peeped into the business room on the camera, she was staring at him through the glass. The good thing is, you can see out but you can't see in. And there's another beauty in there with her."

Pierce nods his head, "I think my bodyguard and I will stay here to watch out for her because I don't trust Adego. Carson, give us a room next to hers."

"She's in the suite; her friend is next door. But for safety purposes, I can't tell the exact room, but I can assure you, you'll be close."

"Good, we can keep an eye on them both."

"Sounds like a plan to me. Give me a few, and I'll bring the key fob back in here."

"Good deal, Carson.

I'm so thankful Carson looks out for and trusts me. Now, all I have to do is summons Brad for some clothes. Didn't have any idea I'd be spending time at The Wellington, but as long as she's here, I'm here.

I close my eyes for a moment. Kate, could it be her? Did you send her to me, my angel?

I retrace my decision to come to The Wellington. The urge to eat dinner here tonight was unshakeable. I even tried to suggest to myself somewhere else to go a couple of times. My mind kept leading me here. I understand why. Mashing the call button on my watch, I wait until Chuck's face appears.

"Yes, sir, Mr. Jansen?"

"Chuck, do you see Adego in the hall?"

"Sir, he got on the elevator, and from the looks of it, he's going to the sixth floor."

"Okay, we are staying at The Wellington a few nights. I'll have Brad pack both of us a bag. Are these changes good with you?"

"Sir, you know I'm cool with whatever. Say the word."

"Thanks, Chuck. Look out, hang out down here until Brad brings our bags."

I disconnected from Chuck and punched the code in my watch to Brad, who answered on the second ring.

"Mr. Jansen, are you alright?"

"Brad, I'm fine."

"You never call me after you leave the office, so when I saw your name, it startled me."

"I need a favor. Would you go to my place and pack Chuck and me a bag. I'm staying at The Wellington Hotel for a few days."

"Okay, but you can spend Christmas with my wife and me if you'd like."

"Thanks, Brad. Your offer warms my heart, but I think I would prefer to stay here. Give your wife, Emily, my love. I'll make sure to bless you for taking care of this matter for me."

"Mr. Jansen, you've blessed us enough. I'll be there shortly."

Brad disconnected the call.

What I appreciate the most from my employees is their

loyalty and the fact they aren't greedy or selfish. They each genuinely love me like family, and I feel the same way. Their love makes it easy for me to go beyond the call of duty to eliminate their struggles.

Kate believed in making sure each of our employees owned homes. And I made sure their children had college funds and teaching them to understood the power to get wealth, using God's principles and precepts.

We all succeed.

But yet, I take none of the glory. The glory alone belongs to God because the reality is, I was doing what a Christian does for his brother. Love him as he loves himself.

Gathering my belongings, I spot Carson coming through the evening crowd to deliver my room key. Right on time. I can shower while Chuck waits on Brad, get dressed, and return to the lounge for a drink.

The Christmas music in the elevator is igniting feelings of joy and sadness. How I wished I had one more Christmas to spend with my Kate. I know it's time to move forward, but I must move strategically in my quest to find fulfillment. One wrong move could change the peace I feel, but I also understand it is better to marry than to burn.

Kate freed me to marry before she took her last breath. She knew my high-strong nature had been suppressed for the entire time she suffered. I could never betray her. Despite her giving me permission to sleep with another, I relied upon God to help me deny my flesh.

I also sit on the side of error. For every time I judged an older man for being with a younger woman, I repent. I realize an older woman can satisfy me, but how willing is she to get pregnant and give birth to a child or two?

I want children more than anything.

I also want to feel the joy of having a wife who wants the same thing. Who's excited to shop for baby clothes and furniture and to allow me to rest my head upon her belly—knowing full well the person inside of her is a part of me.

My quest to find a wife goes deeper than a pretty face and a nice body. I'm in search of the soul connected to my future and legacy, one who loves God as much as I do but is willing to take the scrutiny of being the wife of an older gentleman.

I walk off the elevator deep in my thoughts and almost walk right into the lady who must be the black beauty friend. She's also beautiful.

"Hey—" her stance and face were ready for action.

"Excuse me, ma'am."

She rolled her eyes, "You're excused."

I moved past her, but the stern expression stuck in my head. *Lord, I pray her friend isn't mean.*

CHAPTER 14

P atiently, I wait for Quanie to come back down. Although I am still hiding in the Business Center, I'm hoping and praying ole boy is asleep by now. She needs to hurry up because my stomach's growling and almost sounds as loud as a fart. I wish she'd bring her butt on here.

Quanie comes rushing in, "What are you looking like that for? You know I had to come correct."

"Did it have to take you forever? You know I get mean when I'm hungry." She chuckles, but I'm dead serious.

We walk in the lounge, like two-thirds of Charlie's Angels. All eyes on us. Even the women were staring like someone pulled us off the cover of Essence. The evidence we still have *it*.

I let Quanie pick a table smack dab in the center of the room, and I know she chose this table because she doesn't mind showing her tail. But, hey, these bodies are designed to be seen, and I'm not bold enough to deny the fact God has blessed me.

At this point, I'm so hungry I'd sit at the bar. I'm sideways praising God because we aren't seated a hot minute before the waiter hands us our menus. As I expected, he's back to take our orders and pick up the menus and wasn't even gone five minutes.

"So, what's up with you having a little date?"

"Girl, what, the hot mess I met earlier?" I wouldn't call it a date because one, I didn't get a chance to eat, and two, he'll never be my type.

"And he had you out here dressing like that." She looks around the room and back at me. "Is he here?"

"Honey, I prayed the nut would be sleep. I ain't got time for that." Louisiana comes out, and I think my dress is cute.

"Dang, did you at least give the man a shot? We're supposed to be trying something new. Open yourself up a little."

"Quanie, if I opened myself to that nut, I'd be somewhere praising Buddha drinking Bud Light. It ain't happening." And of course, she rolled her eyes at me but who doesn't care is me. I've played the fool once for the sake of having a man, but never again.

"How about I pick your next date?"

"Here we go. I feel one of your college stunts coming on." Quanie's dead serious.

"Feel what you like. I'm about to help you get out of your own way."

I watch her intently as she's looking around hard. And all the while she's looking, I'm praying. Father, touch this nut in her mind and make her think straight.

After she cased the joint like a private eye, she says, "How about I pick him, and you go out at least once a full date, and you give him a real shot?"

"Okay, if we're gonna play the game like that, I'll pick for you, and you have to do the same thing you're asking of me," I smirk because I know how she hates yielding to her own mess.

"Hold up."

She's waving her hands like she's thinking twice, now.

"I don't have a problem with going out. Remember, I'm the one here to share my cookie and get over this drought."

"There you go with that cookie mess. Keep on, those chocolate chips gonna get your tail in some deep stuff."

I know I'm getting on her last nerve, but who cares. If only I can get her to keep her body to and for herself, I'll be batting a thousand.

"They need to bring your food because you're getting on my nerves already."

I furrowed my brows. I wanted to call Quanie the B-word she calls me, but I kept my composure. "Quanie, your nerves must be already on ten because I'm not doing anything I haven't always done. Now, suck up your wine so you can leave me alone."

"Okay. You said I get to pick your date, and you get to pick mine?"

I know she has something up her sleeves because anything she licks her lips, I'm about to go through hell or have to pay to get out of jail. But little does she know, I got my eyes on her match. He's poised and posted up by the bar like he knows I'm talking about him. It's on and popping. "What's up, Quanie? Come on with it, Boo."

She throws an explicit as always. "You ain't ready. But I got you."

Then there's her sneaky smile, which suggests I'm gonna get more than what I bargained for.

"Sister to sister, my word is my bond." It is the way we issue challenges giving the other no room to weasel out. All I can think about is when she had me stuck under a Q-Dog in college. I ended up with a nut for two years, which turned into absolutely nothing but a sexual entanglement. I suck it up, my gut throbbing, and my mind feels like I need to say, 'No.' But, I trust herb, but this bakery is closed for visitors. I say it despite my better judgment, "Sister to sister, my word is my bond." We shake on it. "Okay, who's going first?"

"I have my pick." Quanie's smiling, and I'm so nervous I feel like I need to pee. "The gentleman over there in the booth. Expensive suit. Salt-n-pepper hair. Fine wine."

I look directly into the eyes of the gentleman she's talking about. By the way, he's looking at me. I feel like I'm being set up. *And isn't he the man I saw earlier who reminds me of Bert Reynolds? That is him.*

"Quanie, are you serious? Dude looks old enough to be my father."

"Yes! Professor, can I please state the facts of your situation?"

Now, I feel like I'm about to crap on myself. Gut bubbling, and if I fart, it's going to be a mess.

"Number one. Your daddy is one can short of a six-pack. His crazy tail will charter a plane and fly to wherever you are and drag your *butt* back to Louisiana. So, you need a man with a backbone."

And this nut keeps looking at the man.

"Number two. You're a college professor, homeowner, own bank account, etcetera, etcetera. We don't need no broke ninjas either."

I'm twitching because I know she's about to give me another dose of bull she thinks is complete logic. Why do I keep letting this girl get me into stuff? I'm a thirty-year-old woman still acting like my sister is holding something over my head. Shut!

"And number three. You need something different, and well, he's about as different as you're going to get."

I was about to protest, but the heifer cut me off.

"And… He's my pick. You have to go."

"You heifer." It's the only word I can come up with carrying the weight of a cuss word. "Quanie, but the man is white. Are you serious?" I know she's into all bwwm crap, but me, I love me some chocolate. My Daddy chocolate and my goals are to have a chocolate husband and chocolate babies.

"Heifer?"

She bursts out laughing. I think my facial expressions are doing the thing right now. Telling everything and every emotion in my mind.

"This is going to be gooooood. And for the record, he's white and old. So yes, I'm serious."

I know my face wearing disdain, and she's over there mocking me like her team won the darn game. Or like she's setting me up for something she already knows about, and I don't.

CHAPTER 15

I put on my Nike leisure suit then think twice about my selection. *What if she's in the lounge?* I don't want to half step, and she thinks I'm not good enough. My mother always told me because we're poor doesn't mean we can't dress for success. She made my brother's and my suits, and we were sometimes dressed better than the rich children at our Catholic school.

I put on my Kiton navy suit with a black v-neck shirt underneath and inspect myself in the mirror—you *look good for an older man, Pierce.* Truth be told, I'm a little like David. I've learned how to encourage myself.

Chuck is already downstairs waiting for me, and he knows where I want to sit. He'll go reserve my table, and then I won't see him for a while, but his eye is always on me. I spray a little Creed on my shirt because a little goes a long way. I slipped my feet into the black Christian Louboutin Greggo, dressy enough to rock with my suit but also right on time for the shirt, and opened my door.

This time, I'm making sure I'm paying attention because I don't want to bump into anyone.

It actually feels good being out. This is the closest I'll ever get to a night on the town unless someone desires a trip to the symphony or a classical musical. But again, I know my place, and nightclubs aren't my speed. Neither are bars, but the lounge here at The Wellington is laid back and sheik.

Most patrons are customers in the hotel, and you'll often see couples more than you would singles. I'm hoping she'll be downstairs tonight because wherever she is, I'm not allowing her to leave until I meet her.

Maybe it's nothing, but perhaps it is.

I'm certainly not one who believes in luck because time and chance happen to us all and simply because there is a God who moves man in the manner of will and according to the matters of man's heart. So, I'm wise enough to believe God has brought her here for this season in her life. If I find in her the qualities and expressions of Him, I will have found my good thing.

I walk through the lounge doors and spot Chuck at my reserved seat with my drink order. I'm not a heavy drinker and choose wine over hard liquor. So tonight, it's red wine Saint-Émilion Château Ausone because I love the taste.

Nodding, I let Chuck know it's okay to enjoy himself, and I sit patiently watching those coming in and going out. The soft sounds of Rachelle Ferrell and Will Downing are perusing over the crowd, and I'm pleased because Jazz without Ferrell or Downing wouldn't be Jazz at all.

I bob my head to the music and think briefly about Kate. She loved dancing, which is what drew me to her in college. If no one else were on the dance floor, Kate was. And she danced like she had soul. Come to find out, her nanny was a black woman who schooled her in all things music.

My major was music, but Kate knew more about music than I could ever know. And each year, she dragged me to New Orleans Jazz Festival, where we'd dance the night away. Of all the Jazz artists in the world, Rachelle Ferrell was her absolute favorite. We collected every album she's put out.

I close my eyes and allow the music to flow through me. I feel this overwhelming feeling to open my eyes, and who do I see coming through the doors? Black beauty and the friend I bumped into earlier. On instinct, I pick up my glass and take a sip of my wine.

The waiter greets them, and each places their order, but they keep talking as if they hadn't seen one another for a while. I wonder, was this a yearly vacation or a quick get-a-way. So many questions floating through my brain. Is she single, or have children? Does she want children? Does she work? If she'd consider moving.

Hold up, man. You're putting the kettle on the pot with no water in it. Their discussion is getting deep because they both make these facial expressions I can't call. At one point, she looked pissed, then happy, then annoyed, and then scared. If I could be a fly sitting on their table.

She's in the same grey dress she had on earlier, and from what Carson said, she stayed right in the Business Center the entire time. Was Adego so out-of-line the woman would hide from him? I feel my rising temperature thinking of what he said to her.

He's coming close to me doing him something, so it's best he gets out of town and soon.

My attention is drawn back towards the table because it appears she likes music. She's swaying to the beat, and I only wish she were in my arms. I love her big curly hair. It's a hair-style a bold woman would wear. I believe Kate called it natural hair.

She tried to school me in black women because she knew I was fascinated with everything about them. How they could be so strong and yet so vulnerable. How they would fight you if you hurt someone they loved, and then turn right around and nurse your wombs if you reached out to them for help.

There was something so intriguing about them, and enticing. And she's a full-figured black woman, which makes it even better. I used to tell Kate men loved all kinds of women, but no matter how big or small a woman was, her confidence and the way she carried herself put her on a man's radar.

Kate had been in all sizes. From eight to sixteen, I appreciated the warmth of her hugs no matter what size she was. Judging by looks, black beauty is a size sixteen, and I'm willing to wrap my arms around every part of her. If she'd let me.

CHAPTER 16

I look over towards his table, and he's taking a drink. He looks to be enjoying the music, but since when were white men into Rachelle Ferrell. Then the fact he's swaying like he has rhythm is tripping me out.

I whisper a prayer. Lord, help me, and please let PawPaw have not one ounce of swag. "Okay, I'm ready." I should pick the guy who's going bald and needs a hair cut, but I reframe from doing what I don't want to be done to me.

"Okay, PawPaw it is." I have to laugh at myself. "Now you, Ms. Thang, see that guy standing over there by the bar looking around like he's casing the joint. That's your cookie monster right there."

"Girl, he's the hotel manager."

She's turning up her nose, and if she declines, we can call the whole deal off. *Say no. Say no. Say no.*

"I give you Daddy Warbucks, and you give me the d— hotel manager. Are you serious?"

"Nawl, nut. The guy standing at the end of the bar with the Armani three-thousand-dollar suit, Boo. Ask me how I know?"

"How do you know?"

"Daniel Terrell Prince wears nothing but the best, and if the hotel manager can afford a darn three-thousand-dollar suit, he's at a point in his life that he can at least smell the cookie."

"Enough with the cookie analogies. What if he's a pick-pocketer or sitting around searching for sugar mammas?"

She's getting antsy, flagging the waiter down, asking for shots. Maybe she'll call the whole deal off, but knowing Quanie, she'll go through with it to one-up me. "Look, if he's the manager, then you can bounce. Deal?" I'm cracking up because if it were hot, she'd be sweating.

"Yeah, whatever, deal. When are we supposed to do this thing?"

She acts as though I'm going to say tomorrow. Heck nawl. If this is going to be done, it's going to be done right now. "All we have is right now. So let's do this."

"Fine. I'm ready when you are."

Let me get a couple more bites of this chicken because I don't need my stomach farting in front of PawPaw." I bite my chicken and chew it, hoping by some small chance she'll have a change of heart, but it looks like she's ready."

"Are you trying to chicken out?"

"No, ma'am, I'm all in, but if he smells like Bengay or says anything about limbs hurting, I'm flying back over here like I have on a Wonder Woman cape."

"He doesn't smell like Bengay. He actually smells quite nice."

Her butt's up to something, wiggling her eyebrows, and I know my face looking some type of way.

"Come on, let's get this over with."

I think twice about what she said. It almost went over my head. "Awe, heck nawl. Wait a minute. Wait. A. Minute. How in the world do you know how he smells?"

"He almost ran me over in the elevator. But he was extremely polite. So, tell PawPaw hi for me."

I pucker my lips together, but I'm ready to get this over with. Worst case scenario, he'll be married, and his wife is on the way. "Okay, but if he's married, no deal."

She sticks out her pinky finger. We pinky pound, sealing our dare with an x. Then she walks her happy little butt towards the bar.

I get up and walk over towards PawPaw, who is staring at me like a mistletoe is hanging over my head.

"Hello, my name is Daiya, and yours."

"Have a seat, Daiya."

"Well, actually, I didn't come to stay. I wanted to know if you'd consider going on a date with me. Nothing major. A quick cup of coffee, and you can go on about your business."

"Oh, really?"

"Yes, but are you married?"

"I haven't even told you my name, and you're already trying to know my business."

I laugh because he shocks me, and two, he said the same thing I was telling the nut earlier. So, I take the seat he's offered me and start over.

"My name is Daiya Prince, and I'd like to take you on a date."

"So, you would?"

"Yes, I would."

"I'm not accustomed to women asking to take me out, but sure. And by the way, I'm Pierce Jansen."

"Okay, Ms. Jansen, it's nice to meet you."

"No, call me Pierce, and I take it as though you and your friend have committed to a dare, and I was the pick for you."

I buck my eyes and know it doesn't pay to lie about anything, so I asked, "How in the world did you know?"

"I've been your age before, and it sort of reminds me of something my brother and I did back in high school."

"So, are you saying we're childish?"

"Actually, I'm feeling quite blessed because whether you know it or not, my plans were to leave this lounge with you in my arms."

"Oh really," I drop my eyes to stare at him. PawPaw doesn't know who he's playing with, and I'm not a sugar cake looking for a Sugar Daddy. "So do tell. How in the world did you figure I'd go anywhere with you?"

"I didn't, but I surely wasn't going to allow the opportunity to pass me up. Now, how do you feel about taking a walk with me?"

"Pierce, I'm not sure about leaving here with you. I met you."

"Daiya, you've been knowing me all of your life. Have you ever heard of the story of Leah and Rachel?"

Now, he has my attention for real. Is he throwing the Bible at the P. K.? I'll play dumb to the fact to see where he's going. "Yes, I have. And the idea of a man being with my sister first and then me is not what's up."

"Okay, so I need you to see it from my perspective. My wife, Kate, always knew I was created with a passionate desire to love a black woman. She also knew I was faithful to her until the day she died. Now, you do know the Lord, and in reality, you are Kate's sister."

"Okay, what Bible have you been reading, and are you crazy?"

"I read the Holy Bible, and the true and living God is my Father."

"Okay, but where did the spin-off of this story come from?"

"I asked my Father for a wife, and He gave me Kate (Leah). He knew I always wanted Daiya (Rachel), but He also knew Kate would teach me some things Daiya couldn't. He knows the ends and outs of His plan and what He's purposed for each of us. Do you care to hear more?"

I simply nod.

"I would never betray Kate, nor would I ever touch Daiya, until Kate was resting with the Father. There's a reason you came to New York when you did. Now, Daiya (my Rachel), since Leah is gone, I can eagerly marry, take care of, and plant my generational seeds in you. This goes deeper than you can see, Daiya. But for five months, I've patiently waited for you."

"Pierce, you are full of it. Is this some old man spill you've been waiting to pour on some ignorant little black girl?"

"You are not a girl, and I don't play with God. 'The visible marks of extraordinary wisdom and power appear so plainly in all the works of the creation that a rational creature who will but seriously reflect on them cannot miss the discovery of a deity.'"

"Quoting John Locke, huh?"

"Yes, it was, but you knew? Don't answer. I don't play with God, use His name in vain, nor trust in His power for foolishness. Daiya, the moment you sat in front of me until now, you've got the truth of this matter."

"Wait a minute. Pierce, you are taking me too fast. Are you a prophet?"

"No, I'm not a prophet, but I am a prayer."

"Okay, so how serious are you about prayer?" If he tells me once a week or over his food, I will get up from this table so fast and get ghost—a natural repeat.

"Daiya, I pray three times a day. At nine, three, and again at nine. Would you care to join me tomorrow?"

"Sure, I'm not afraid to pray."

"Okay, so why don't we start our date with prayer, and then I'll have Carson to let us use the movie room to watch a private film of your choice."

"Who is Carson?"

"Carson Wellington. I thought your friend knew him because she's over there talking to him right now."

I want to jump up right then and there to tell Quanie he's

not the bellhop. But I also didn't want to appear like we were groupies scouting out the club's richest men. Good Lord, I knew this was going to backfire on us one way or another. Darn, Quanie.

"He's the one who had Deacon to come to get me from the airport? I think they've talked a time or two."

"Did Deacon pick you up in a black SUV?"

"Wellington's personal vehicle, huh? See, again, I think this situation has God all over it."

"Give me a few. Let me speak to Quanie, and I will walk with you. Do I need to get a big coat?"

"No, we're going right next door, and the walk will only take one to two minutes."

"Okay, why don't you meet me at the front door."

CHAPTER 17

I walk over to our table and put my jacket on. Picking up my crossbody, I pull it over my head and look back over my shoulder to see if Pierce is watching me.

He is. Shut.

One mind wanted to put a couple more pieces of chicken in my mouth, but Momma always said, 'If you leave food or drink on a table unattended, you never go back to it.' I'm following the rules.

I adjust my jacket and purse and then go over to where Quanie is talking to Carson. Hopefully, if I call him by name, nut-nut will pick up on it.

"Well, hello Quanie and Carson Wellington. How is this little chat going?" She's probably too tipsy because she doesn't even react to what I said. But why does she jump like I'm the police or something? I know she's over here saying or doing something she has no busy doing.

Carson sits forward as if he's ready to hear something of interest, and she's sitting there in dreamland plundering.

I got to give it to her. She recovered like a champ. "Fine. And what about you and," She whispers, "PawPaw?"

I roll my eyes and keep batting them so she can think about what I've said, "He's definitely on another level, and I'm beginning to think he's too much like my Dad. The dude got me feeling like the woman at the well encountering Jesus. Come see a man who's telling me all about myself."

"Dad, Jesus, and a Bible parable in the same sentence. This calls for sisterly intervention. Carson, thank you for your time. I think we should call it a night."

Oh, she thinks she's slick standing up and trying to spin her little tail away, but I ain't having it. I know her too darn well.

This is where the big girl blocks her like we're joined at the hip, "So Carson, where are you two going on your date tomorrow?"

"He's not interested. Come on and tell me about the woman at the well again. Night Carson."

She says, and he furrows his brow as if this is his first time hearing about the date. But Carson peeps right through her game, too, and for the first time ever, I think she's found her match. He runs his hands over his chin, "I'll have to plan something special. How about I pick you up at 7?"

I stand beside them, quiet, watching all of the heated banter between the two of them.

I'm all on top of her shiznyee (another one of my alternative words to keep me from cussing). "No, you might as well stay right here and work out the details with Carson because this woman at the well is taking a walk next door with Pierce. What in the heck is next door, only God knows. And Yes, Carson, seven tomorrow is going to be perfect for her." I answer and watch Quanie almost pee on herself.

She's rolling her eyes so hard, but Carson is looking thoroughly entertained by our discussion.

Quanie looks at Carson as if she wants him to bail and then so candidly reminds him of a conference he's having. Then she acts like she's concerned about pulling him away from his obligations. Her angonna is trying to wiggle her way out of this date, but he's not budging.

Carson smiles, "You're correct, but I'd be remiss to miss the opportunity to have you alone."

I laugh, knowing full well Carson has put her tush in a sling. But if looks could kill, she'd have me hung up on a tree. Quanie can create the games and the rules, but it is hard as heck for her to follow the plan. She was the same way in college. Always trying to fix my life with these crazy schemes but hating when stuff backfired on her. And it often did.

Quanie looks at me with daggers flowing from her eyes to mine. "Don't you have a walk by the well?"

"I surely do. And enjoy your dinner date tomorrow." I laugh because I got her tail. Knowing her, she's been lying the whole entire time like she was over there for me. Not working this time. "Carson, enjoy your date, and I'll see you later, Ms. Cookie Monster."

I twitch right on to the front door where Pierce is waiting on me. She's going to get enough of playing with me when the game keeps backfiring on her. I'm so tickled, I can barely keep my composure.

"What's got you so tickled?"

"One day, I'll explain it all to you, but now, I would like to focus on where you plan on taking me."

"Come on. Is it okay for me to hold your hand?" Pierce asks, and I agree.

What could be wrong with him holding my hand? We walk next door, and when he opens the door, I'm as memorized as I was the first moment I step foot into The Wellington Hotel.

It is absolutely breathtaking.

The chandelier and staircase look like something from a Hollywood movie. A couple of people are listening and dancing to a live band playing music. And Pierce takes me straight to the dance floor.

"May I have this dance?"

"Why sure?"

We dance to *With A Christmas Heart* by the late Luther Vandross.

Darn, this man has so much swag, and he can dance his butt off. How the heck did a white man get so much rhythm and finesse?

I hang on to each note Pierce is singing in my ear. And with each twirl, I feel like a princess who has been found by her prince—Nawl *girl. Quit tripping. You just met PawPaw. But he's dancing like he's my age.*

Pierce has to be every bit of six-one because I'm five-nine, and he still has perfect height over me. He's holding me with one arm and lifts my chin with his free hand.

"Penny for your thought."

"I was thinking about your height."

He chuckles. "Is that a problem for you?" Not unless my weight is a problem for you.

"Your weight?"

"Yes, all my adult life, my mother has reminded me I need to watch my weight."

"How do you feel about your weight?"

"I love where I am. I think it fits me fine."

"My sentiments exactly. Daiya, as long as you love Daiya, it doesn't matter what anyone thinks or says. I'm happy with your body the way it is."

The band must be into Vandross Christmas music because now their singer is singing an excellent rendition of *Every Year, Every Christmas*. And Pierce knows the entire song. He's singing in my ear. I'm feeling like this will be our song for the rest of our lives.

This man can sing.

I break the silence. "You have a beautiful voice. Are you a singer?"

He laughs. "Only if you want me to be. For the world, no. My college major was music, but I have a Ph. D. in business."

"Which explains the awesome voice and the savvy businesslike way you've dealt with me."

"Listen, this is not a deal, or let's make a deal. What I'm presenting to you is a lifetime. Now, tell me a little more about you."

"I'm a college professor, and I'm from Louisiana."

"You must be from north Louisiana because I hear more country than I do Louisiana drawl."

"You're actually correct. I live on the outskirts of Shreveport, and I teach at a local college."

CHAPTER 18

The conversation stops, and Pierce holds me tighter. My body is throwing all types of signals to my brain. It's been so long since a man has danced with me. Heck, even held me in his arms. A church hug or two over the years, but never in this manner.

And indeed, never staring into my eyes like he wants me.

The more I look at Pierce, he does remind me of Mr. Reynolds, but his body is so firm and tight. I feel his thigh muscles against mine, and he's probably got only one percent of body fat.

Lord, I'm feeling a little too comfortable. Please don't let me get so swept away. I forget I'm a closed bakery. My body is reacting to this man Jesus, and you promised to provide an escape for me. But, give me the escape in my mind, not from this moment, in Jesus' name.

I sigh.

"Are you alright, Daiya?"

"Yes, Pierce, I'm alright. Tell me more about you."

"I own this building, and several more in this great state. I also own a brokerage, am a contractor, and own a music studio and label. I love music, and the artist I represent have become more like family."

"Did you and your wife have any children?"

"I told you you'll be the woman who gives me my legacy. You don't believe me?"

"It's not that I don't believe you. It's that I've just met you, and you're already talking about knocking me up. You've never touched me, don't know me from Eve, and I find it strange that you are coming on so strong."

"I find it strange that you don't understand the providence of God. I also think you're intimidated because you set the tone or not, and I'm coming in the situation setting the atmosphere, and you're afraid. And by the way, I know you from Eve, but as Adam knew her, I know you. I haven't been searching for a wife, because Daiya, I've been waiting for you. I know wife material when I see it, so consider yourself as found."

It takes me a while to answer back because I'm literally thinking. At this point, I will take the advice I give my students, always find ways to ask the questions, and don't pretend as if you know everything. So, I do what any woman in my position would do. I shut up and start dancing.

I dance even harder when the band changes the tempo and begins to sing PJ Morton's version of *This Christmas*. Sounds from sweet Louisiana have followed me to New York, and Pierce is jamming as hard as I am.

I'm laughing so hard because this dude has swag. I'm throwing these hips, and he's catching every move, every step, and he's not missing a beat. I turn with my butt into him, and I feel his stern package up against me: wrong *move, Daiya. Turn around.* And like a bad nightmare, someone taps my shoulder. I turn around, and it's Dareek.

"May I have this dance?" He asks me, but he's looking at Pierce like he's an old man who needs to be in bed by now.

I look at Pierce, and I see his jaws clench under his

beautiful salt and pepper beard. His eyes said, no and my heart says, no man will ever disrespect him in my presence.

"I'm sorry, Mr. Adego, but I'm here with Pierce."

He takes my hand in his. "So, you're dissing me for PawPaw?"

"No, I'm dismissing you for My Sugar Daddy." I snatch my hand from his and turn back to Piece. "Can we go now?"

"Your wish is my command." Pierce gives Adego a look saying, try me, and he grabs me by my waist and leads me through the crowd.

I saw this huge man standing by us. It looks like he flew from the ceiling because I never saw him come up. But as Pierce and I are leaving, the same guy is walking sort of behind us.

I whisper. "Pierce, this big guy is following us. I hope you know how to fight."

"I know how to fight in four different ways; boxing, kick-boxing, judo, and taekwondo. Do I need more ways for you?"

"I know, beat your tail with my shoe and spray you with this mace. Is my way good enough for you?"

Pierce starting laughing so hard, he was bending over. He's laughing like a nut, and I'm worried about the old boy who is less than fifty feet behind us.

"Chuck, Chuck, you better run because baby ready to mace you." Pierce is laughing and hollering at the big guy who's now laughing too.

"What's so funny, Pierce? And who the heck is Chuck?"

"Baby, Chuck is my bodyguard."

"Hello, Ms. Prince. I'm Chuck," he extended his hand to shake my hand.

"You all better stop playing with me because my Dad taught me the bigger they are, the harder they fall. Chuck, you were about to get a Louisiana butt whooping."

He and Pierce started laughing so hard they both were in tears.

"Well, Bossman, I'm glad to know she's got your back. I like Ms. Prince. She's all good in my book."

"Chuck, I'm going to marry this woman. Any woman who will defend me and call me her Sugar Daddy is worth being showered with all the love, gifts, and prayers this Sugar Daddy can give." They laughed, and this time I joined in.

There was no way I was going to let Dareek talk down on Pierce or me. He was canceled the moment he let me know he didn't believe in Jesus. And there was no way I'd ever let someone talk down on my Lord and get away with it. I don't care if he were the most impoverished Jew in the city. That Jew went to Calvary on my behalf. He didn't look down on me as the filth and rags I was, and I will let no one bash Him in my presence.

"Daiya, I had Chuck to order us some food and send it to my room. If you're not sleepy, we can have it brought to your room, and we can sit and talk. Any objections or questions?"

"Were you watching us hard and long enough to know I barely ate my food?"

"I sure was. I couldn't figure for the life of me why you all were talking and barely touching your food. Then when you put those two bites in your mouth, chewed fast, and came over to me, I knew the dare was taking you from your food."

"Pierce, what are you trying to do? Make me fall in love with you?"

"I surely am, and Daiya, rarely does anything get past me. When you see this eyebrow go up, watch out. It means I'm trying to figure out the dynamics or circumstances surrounding a particular situation. And yes, I'm absolutely being nosey and all up in your business." We start to laugh.

"You know you answered my next question, don't you?"

"Of course. I saw your facial expression, and I've already

figured out you can't hide anything. Your facial expressions will give you away every time. Now, I have to study you more to find out what facial expression goes with which emotion."

"It's not that serious, Pierce."

"Yes, it is when I want to know everything there is to know about you. So, will it be your room with me or without me?"

"I'm not sleepy, and I'm hungry. It's my room. Nothing else is on your mind, right?"

"I'd be lying if I said, 'no.' I've been wanting to kiss those lips since you walked past me earlier today going to meet Adego."

"It was you? Wasn't it?"

CHAPTER 19

The last three days have been a complete whirlwind. Pierce has taken me to see his 7th Ave office and his condo. We've shopped at every boutique I had on my list, and I haven't had to spend one dime of my own money.D

It's the night of Carson's big Christmas Eve Bash, and I've decided to wear the black party dress. I love the way it fits my hips and still shows the beauty of my legs and waistline. I also am finally feeling comfortable with all of my back out to the tip of my butt.

I mentioned to Pierce I needed a pair of earrings to go with my outfit, and he bought me some black diamond teardrop earrings, a bracelet, and a necklace set. It must've cost him a pretty penny, and although I was a little hesitant, he persuaded me to accept it but as my Christmas gift.

The best Christmas gift anyone has ever given to me. Even Daddy.

I called my parents to wish them a Merry Christmas before I left and to tell Mom all about Pierce. She said she figured someone was smiling up in my face because I haven't called her every day all day as I did on my other trips.

The fact he's older and caucasian, I didn't care to reveal. Quanie's plan to give me something different was shaping into something I've always wanted and needed. So nothing else mattered to me.

As I was willing to stand up to Adego, I'll defend Pierce to my Daddy and the world.

Every moment I spend with Pierce, I realize I've found what I have been missing. We laugh at the same jokes, we finish one another's sentences, and I love to hear his stories about Kate. She seemed to be a wonderful person, and I love that Pierce doesn't make me feel like I'm competing with her.

He's so accepting of me. I don't have to be anyone but me. Sometimes, I talk as country as a bumpkin, and he's alright with the laid back me. He's even had the chance to see the professional me in action, and he seems to love all parts of me.

I'm dressed and waiting for him to knock on my door. Tonight, he is going to see another piece of me. I flat ironed my curly hair, put a part in the dead center, and I'm wearing it completely straight.

Sometimes it even shocks me how long my hair is, and tonight, a little more, and it would have covered my entire back. So I split it towards the back and bring both sides to the front. It's adorable if I say so myself.

I finally hear the knock, and I open the door. Pierce stares at me.

Not like he's upset, I changed my hair. But like he's mesmerized with the woman staring back at him. He doesn't say one word but pulls me into his arms and kisses me with passion and intensity, almost too much for me to handle. In the last few days, I've mastered the art of embracing the escape, but I don't know how much longer I can tempt God or myself.

I free myself from his strong embrace, pick up my clutch, and lay my hand gently on his chest. I remind him our friends are waiting for us.

Pierce may be older, but every part of him is working and ready if you know what I mean. I have to respect the fact our touch is electrifying, and it's not a one-way current.

It's been years for him and me, which is a recipe for disaster, but he respects my decision to wait for marriage. He would have married me yesterday if I would've agreed to it. But, I must be sure I'll love him through sickness and in health, whether we are rich or poor, and until death does us apart.

But, by the looks of us, he's healthier than me. I'm not trying to make him twice widowed, so I have to be sure I'm ready to get Daiya together.

Pierce makes me want to be healthy. He makes me love happiness and the space I'm in.

I smile at him, and he grabs my hand and pulls me gently back into our earlier embrace. He kisses me again. Then my nose, my forehead, and now my neck. And I'm sinking deeper and deeper.

"Baby, we have to go. Pierce, our friends, are waiting for us."

"And Daiya, I'm waiting for you. But, I have to be able to express my emotions in some type of way. No pressure, I want you. All of you, Daiya, will you marry me?"

I look in his eyes to see if he's earnest.

He's dead serious.

"Pierce, I don't know how what…"

He puts his finger to my lips. "Baby, we don't have to work out the logistics. Everything will fall exactly where it needs to fall. I need to know if you will be my wife."

"Are you sure?"

"Daiya, I'm positive. I'm so positive," Pierce went down on one knee and pulled the most enormous and prettiest diamond ring out of his pocket Daiya had ever seen. "Now, I'm only going to ask you one more time tonight. Daiya Treshelle Prince, will you marry me."

"Yes, Pierce Jansen, I will." He pulls me, and I'm sitting on his knee as he kisses me. Then he slides the rock on my finger. It fits me perfectly. I wished it would have put a rope over all of my thoughts and slung them out of my mind.

I stand, and Pierce stands up and hugs me as if I was planning on running away from him with this rock. I hung onto him so tight he could feel my heartbeat.

In such a short time, Pierce has taken me from low self-esteem to complete confidence. In my God, myself, and in what I have to offer. All the times my family has said, "You getting big, but you are still so pretty," and I thought they were complimenting me. He's wiped the sting away.

Every time someone's said, "Your hair is pretty natural, but you should perm it." Or the infamous, "I like your hair better straight." He's complimented the pain of other's opinions away. And no one knows how deep it cuts to have your body, hair, and skin always the subject of someone else's concern.

It can be so depleting.

But yet, I've learned how to function through all the hurt of their scrutiny. In four days, this man has taken the sting away and made me see myself through the eyes of God. How is it you can live around people your entire life—who claim to love you more than anyone—but daily, they chip away at your resolve? They make you question everything you'd like to think about yourself, and their isms slowly incorporate as your issues.

Tonight, I'm holding the hand of the man who God sent to break every chain and stronghold my family and church folks have caused me to embrace. I'm accepting Daiya Treshelle Prince the way I am. And the only thing I'm looking forward to changing is my desire to seek God through prayer.

Pierce and I have prayed together three times a day, and it's been so refreshing. It's transforming my mind. I'm breaking chains of conformation and word curses, and the transformation of my mind is renewing me.

Oh, what peace I have.

We step off the elevator, and this time it's me who pulls him in for a kiss. In front of everyone watching, I kiss this man making sure he's stamped, Daiya. He appreciates by kissing me with much passion, and it feels darn good.

This night couldn't be more perfect.

The only bad thing Quanie is allowing Carson to take a previously arranged date to the party, and she's decided not to come. What a crazy idea? There's no way I would have let her make an agreement so silly. No way.

CHAPTER 20

We have been seated at the best table in the place. I'm cheerful, but at the same time, a little perturbed. I'm mugging this chick Carson sat by us, who is his date for tonight. I can't blame anyone except Quanie for this mess. I pick up my phone and text her.

My first thought was to see where the heck she was. I put on a front long enough to snap a picture of Lena and Carson together. As if he—with her—is worthy of even a little of my photo space. Little do they know, it's a set-a-fire-photo, and in five minutes, Quanie better be lighting the match.

Lena might have had a decent night if she would have dressed appropriately, but the dress she wore screamed lap-dance, no panties. But not on my watch. I'll snatch her so fast; she'll lose those blonde tracks.

Pierce touched me, and he smiles. I know he's trying to soften my expression. My face.

I must have been mugging Lena real hard. But I like how he thinks he knows me. He's convincing me—he does.

But, why has Carson left her again like quitting a bad habit? Right before this little photo-fire, we'd been sitting here for well over thirty minutes, and he hadn't been back yet. Quanie better get her crap together. This is not babysitting Carson night. I'm trying to dance myself into Christmas.

The piano player starts playing, and by the first keys, I know this band is about to play my jam. I jumped up and pulled Pierce by the hand before the singer sings the first lyrics. As soon as she sings, "I want to run away with you," I look deep into Pierce's eyes. Baby, this is my song to you.

He pulls me closer until there is no gap between us—our bodies in sync. As much as this is a physical display of our connection, more in-depth. Spiritual. We carve our little section and dare anyone to step in our path. The dance is so passionate. I open my eyes to find the room standing still and staring at us. Neither of us cares. I lift my hand and rub the back of Pierce's head.

His body trembles.

And he kisses me. Deep enough to relax his body, sufficiently ignites mine, and long enough to mark a moment in time to share forever.

I feel like I've stepped into an episode of Dancing With The Stars, but the contestants are lovers. He dips me, and I'm safe in his arms. Pierce pulls me back up, and our lips touch again, but he whispers, "Daiya, you'll never be alone again."

"Pierce," I whisper as tears capture a place in our moment, and lay my head in the locks of his shoulder. I feel so safe, like no one else in the world matters, and he's exactly what I've been missing.

Pierce kiss my eyes and whispers, "Baby, explore the world with me. Marry me tomorrow, Daiya. Whatever we face, we face it together."

"I will, Pierce." He twirls me out and then brings me back into him, but this time, the back of my body rests in him, and my right arm goes up, and as soon as my hand touches his chin, he twirls me out and brings me back face to face with him.

The song seems to go on forever. And I don't mind at all. I'm right here where I want and need to be, and I'm never going anywhere unless he's going with me.

For the first time, I'm making a grown woman decision for Daiya. I don't care who approves and who doesn't. All I care about is this man, right here, never leaving me to face the world alone.

Pierce pulls me in and whispers, "I'm not going to leave you, Daiya." As if he's reading my thoughts, and when the band is ending our song, My Song by H.E.R., I can't help but feel blessed.

The crowd is clapping and congratulating us. I guess the massive diamond on my finger is the only announcement I need. And if strangers can see, we were made to be together, which is more than enough confirmation for me. Pierce escorts me back to our table, and I'm snatched up so quick I almost stumble.

"Bish…" Quanie calls me.

But as promised, Piece catches me from falling. All our beautiful dancing and this heifer about the ruin the perfect evening by making me fall; leave it to disgruntled in New York. But I'm so happy she's finally brought her tail down to spend the evening with us. We both squeal. A little softer than when we first met here, but not soft enough to not cause a scene. My girl came like fire. Quanie has breast, naval, and thigh working at the same time. Hot girl, no disclaimer.

"Oh my god, Daiya, I'm so happy for you."

"You probably think—"

"It doesn't matter what I think, boo. Pierce put a ring on it." We wave our hands like we're Beyonce. "Did you tell your parents?"

"Not yet. I'm still adjusting to everything. So, we're going to Pierce's lake house. Will you be okay in the city alone?" I ask her because all she has to do is say, 'no,' and it's a wrap. Either

I'll stay, or she's going with me. But something tells me there's so much more to the story.

"What's wrong?" I asked her.

"Do you see Carson?"

"Yeah, he's right there."

I point him out at the front of the room, talking with a small group. He's staring at Quanie, she's staring at Carson, and I'm wondering what is going on.

"Quanie, I have my mace, and Pierce knows karate."

She snickers. "So, you're going to mace someone at a Christmas party?"

"Girl, I don't know these people. But if someone has beef with you, they have beef with me."

Now, I'm looking over at Carson like he's done me something. And like Pierce, Quanie knows how to soften my resolve.

"Thank you for taking this crazy-ass adventure with me."

I soften and smile at her. "You are my girl. Heck nawl, it's deeper than that. You're my one and only sister. Who else would I roll with if not you? Girl, we roll until the wheels fall off—four flat tires and on squealing metal if we have to. Quanie, if you go, I go. If you say, 'No,' I say, 'No.' But for some reason, I feel in my heart, Quanie, tonight, it's time for you to say, 'Yes.' But if I need to lay these paws on Carson, you know I will."

"Nah, I f'ed up, and I have to make this right."

"We need a real conversation the moment you get back home."

"It's a date. Love you, and congratulations."

We hug, holding each other tight. What an adventure? I'm engaged, and I know without a doubt, Quanie's in love. "Love you too, Sissy," I tell her wanting to say more, but we're rudely interrupted.

"Hello, gorgeous. Can I have this dance?" Adego, with his thick African accent, comes rolling up behind Quanie.

Before I knew it, I cussed, "Oh hell no!"

I shocked Quanie and Pierce. Then I looked at my sister, "Girl, it's a long story."

"I'm not talking to you, but her," Adego persists.

Both of our stances changed. I see Pierce and Chuck walking fast from the bar, but before either of us could jump down his throat—cause we were going for the juggler—Quanie's Santa Claus appeared.

"Nah, man. You can't." The cold tone in Carson's voice captures all of our attention.

"Look." Dareek Adego counters.

And this time, it's Quanie who tells him she's with Carson. I smile because now I know she's where God wants her to be. Although Pierce and I are ready to leave, I watch her and Carson dance together, leaving nothing for our imagination. And if Lena doesn't see what we see, shame on her.

CHAPTER 21

Her warm body next to me is more than enough for me. I respect she's making me wait until we get married, but last night, it took all the restraint in me not to allow my hands to roam her beautiful body. I rubbed her hair, hoping she'll awaken, but she shifts and falls deeper. I have to move around before temptation gets the best of me.

I see now, one of the differences between us, I'm an early riser, and Daiya's going deeper at six a.m. I slide out of bed, put on my robe and my slippers. I'll bring her breakfast and coffee in bed.

It's Christmas morning, and although we didn't arrive at my lakefront property until three in the morning, I'm well-rested and ready to get this show on the road. Daiya promised to become my wife today, and I'm making it happen. What's the use in waiting? Calvin Richardson's song *Can't Let Go* is playing on the radio, and I promise I'm not letting go.

I'm not getting any younger, and the way things are going in the world, we may as well be happy and enjoy life. What I plan on doing—enjoying Daiya for the rest of our lives.

I brought her to the home I shared with Kate so I could

introduce her to my past. I wanted to see how she'd feel about me selling the property and then searching for her and my new home. Heck, Pierce, you don't even know if she willing to live in New York. Either way, everything about this house screams Kate and our families.

Suitable for the old me. But now I need a change of scenery. I need to discover what I like apart from Kate, but with Daiya. Even last night, I found myself smitten with her all over again. She made me feel so good when we arrived until I'm still relishing in the joy I've seen. This woman made me feel like Kate was welcoming her into our family.

Our conversation, her compliments, my contentment, and how grateful she is has solidified my choice. No, God's will.

I watched Daiya as she looked at all the photos asking me to name who was who. What surprised me was, I didn't have to tell her who was Kate. Even with my cousin's photo right next to Kate's, Daiya knew who was who. She pointed her out as if they'd been friends in another world or something.

And me, for the first time since Kate passed, I was able to stand even the thought of sleeping in this house. Walking through it frustrates me, but not this morning.

Her commiseration and empathy towards me—her consideration— she cradled me, and for the first time since Kate's passing, someone gave me room to share about the last four years of Kate's life.

It took resiliency to endure what I endured, but no one patted me on the back or even hinted acknowledged my good job. The only thing Kate's parents cared about was getting her remains back to Texas, and my parents only cared about making sure Kate's parents could take nothing from me.

It seemed to outsiders my wife was running everything, but what they didn't remember is I was the business major. I worked my butt off so Kate could be the queen of our business, and I gave her room to spread her wings. I never tried to stop her from doing anything she wanted to do. I pushed her. But because of how her family felt about me, Kate and I made sure my name was first on everything. Trust.

The year before she passed, Kate suggested selling her portions of ownership to me, and she could do whatever she wanted with the money, which was fine with me. I bought her out of everything we owned: the construction company, real estate brokerage, music label, rental properties, and even my music studio. I'm now the sole owner of everything and have been for almost two years.

In her will, Kate and I divided the twenty-one-million-dollars in three ways. With me, her parents, and her scholarship foundation. I paid the attorney to do the paperwork and paid him cash so we each could get a clear seven million. We also made sure to put in a clause giving me the power to revoke her parent's seven million if they did anything to disrespect me.

See, Kate had my back. And even in death, I have hers. I will do as she asked me, even if her parents act a fool. I'm going to make sure her final wishes are made.

I gave Daiya permission to ask whatever she wanted to ask. And like I knew it would, the question came up if we were moving too soon. I knew it was time to share with her a video from my Kate.

Hello, beautiful one. I know you are because my Pierce loves beauty. Please take care of him for me. He loves to love, and he's such a faithful and generous man who deserves to be loved. Give him all the things I wasn't able to give. He's probably going to want more babies than you can imagine, but I know you won't be alone. God has brought you into his life for a reason, and if you're watching this tape, I know the wedding is soon. Whether it's a day after my death or months, he's been the perfect gentleman, and it's time for him to move on. It's time for my Pierce to live finally. He's one of a kind. Stop blushing, Pierce.

I was blushing and crying.

Also, know Pierce, and I fast and prayed for you. I wanted God to be so involved, Pierce would know you from the moment he looked at you. He'd know I've been in Heaven, carefully praying and kneeling before God's throne, asking Him to orchestrate so wherever you were in the world, He would lead you to Pierce. If that's what we can do in Heaven. LOL.

God did, and I'm thankful. He's always loved, black women. Don't smile and blush, Pierce.

If you are a black woman by God's design, please tell him soul food isn't the only thing black people can cook. And by all means, please let Pierce know the ends and out about styling your hair because he has driven me crazy asking all my blacks friends about their hair.

Thanks for trusting the God in me to take the time to watch this video. I can undoubtedly rest well, knowing our Pierce is finally getting all the love he's given. And, don't mind Chuck, Matt, or Carson. These guys are the closest we have to sons, and Pierce would give either of them his last.

Back to Pierce. I fell in love with him the day I met him, and you've probably done the same thing. If not the same day, probably the next day. He's too generous, kind, gentle, meek, and humble not to love. The fruits of the spirit are overflowing in him, and he makes you love him. Don't be afraid. Allow yourself to love a man who will be faithful until death.

Much Love,

Kate Jansen

By the time the video ended, both Daiya and I were crying, and for the first time since I've been a grown man, I called another woman mine. My Daiya. And to respect her, we slept in the guest room. She even talked me out of putting a for sale sign in the yard today. She cautioned me to wait until I had fully dealt with all things Kate and promised to be by my side through it all.

I'm so blessed.

Not only did God blessed me with one wonderful wife, but He's also exceeded Himself again.

I know it's a God thing because Daiya even has me cooking. I haven't so much as even boiled an egg since Kate's passing. I cooked every day for her, and when she died, I hung up the mitts and utensils.

But look at me this morning.

Dancing around this kitchen like I'm Suzy Homemaker. Then, I also have one last thing to prove to Kate; I can cook for a black woman. I made grits, homemade biscuits, bacon, sausage, eggs, and cut up some fruit. There was enough food here to feed an army, but Chuck will take care of his plate and the leftovers. He's a big guy.

CHAPTER 22

I move my body and then throw my hand to feel him, but he's gone. I open my eyes, and on the vast wall clock, I see it's already eight. Dang Daiya, you sleeping late in New York like you don't have a job when you go back home.

What will I do?

Pierce has entirely too many businesses in New York to leave, and although my contract is over in May, how in the world will I tell Daniel Prince I'm leaving The Christian Love Assembly. Daddy will do two flips and three cartwheels. *Lord, work this out for me.*

I stretched. Hopefully, pulling away from the thought of going home as Mrs. Jansen. I need to just enjoy the moment. Problem-free. I get up and dig around in my bag.

There it is. My hairbrush. This is one of the reasons I rarely straighten it—hair is everywhere. I pull it all up in a high pony-tail and shake my head from side to side to make sure it's flowing right. Another reason why I rock my curls. They can be all wild and all over the place, and people still say they're cute. This straight hair will rat up like a bird's nest if I don't bring it under subjection with hairspray or gel.

I go to the restroom to wash my face and brush my teeth. I'm sort of glad Pierce didn't see all these eye boogers I have. Not to mention this line of crusted slob running from my lips to my cheek.

I must've been too darn comfortable. But sleeping in a comfortable be with a man is lovely. And the mattress is better than mine on a good day. I snicker. The big difference between black and white folks is not our skin, but totally how we spend coins.

We buy stuff to make us look good, and they purchase crap to make them sleep well.

And to think this is a guest bed.

Shut, I can only imagine what his main bed feels like. But, I protested against sleeping here, thinking I'd have to sleep in their bed. Kate's resting in heaven, and in my book, so is her bed. She may as well have packed it and took it with her because Daiya is not lying, sitting, or even looking at her bed or even going in her room.

I'm going to respect the dead. Period.

I told Pierce to keep the house, but this is my first and last night staying here. He and Kate were close, and although I don't expect his memories to die, I won't be creating any with him in the home they shared the most of everything in.

After watching her video, he and I both cried like God had given us permission through Kate to love again. Kate had enough love for Pierce to convince another woman he is the best man on earth.

Too late, Kate. I already put him on my heart's pedestal after comparing him to the last man I gave my heart to. The sucker dogged me out so bad, I promised God my bakery would only bake cookies for the one who put a rock on my finger and gave me his last name.

Pierce was halfway there.

I spent three years chasing a man who seriously considered

me as his main girl, but never his only girl. Quanie and I had more fights about him, with his side chicks, than I care to even admit. And the fact he married one of them tripped me out. I'm glad her dumb angonna took my spot on his hotbed.

The last I heard, he made her participate in some swinging events, and they both are now HIV positive. Lord, knows it could, would, and probably should have been me except the grace of God. But one thing for sure, it became all the motivation I needed to stay celibate. Nine years and later, and I'm still celibate.

Last night, I will not lie. I thought about going there a couple of times. Then, when Pierce got close enough to me to feel his package, I started praying. I don't know what made me think a man almost fifty wouldn't be packing anything. I see now. It's all in how he spreads himself. And from the feel, Pierce hasn't been spreading himself at all.

Shaking my head, I try to pull my thoughts out of the gutter. You do what you think, and if you allow yourself to become trapped in your mind, you'll eventually be trapped in your actions. I'm missing something. And now I know exactly what it is. Pierce and I have prayed together every day this week. I guess he called himself giving me a break this morning. This the morning I need it the most.

I go back towards the bed and fall on my knees.

"Father, I thank you for this vacation. I did not expect to be found, nor did I come here looking. But Father, I sure am glad. You had someone waiting for me. Teach me how to be the recipient of his love, to be the wife he needs, and to constrain my flesh and fix everything I'm afraid of. I know you did not bring us together for me to allow fear to drive us apart. I love you, Lord. And thank you for Kate's very life. I'm so blessed by her wanting Pierce and me to live and be happy. Lord, You are awesome, and only You could do this. I love and praise You, in Jesus' name. Amen."

I get up off my knees and dry my eyes. I sure seem to be crying at the drop of a pin lately. I grabbed my makeup bag, put on a little eyeliner and some pink lip gloss. I know he's cooking breakfast because I smell bacon. It doesn't make any sense for me to show up looking like I had a war with the pillow, so I rummaged through my bag to find something cute and comfy to put on. It's Christmas, and at the Prince house, I'd be dressed already and helping mom warm up food for our twelve o'clock brunch.

I miss my parents. I grab my phone and tell Siri to dial Momma. It took her until the third ring to answer, kind of normal. She's either cooking or warming food, and I miss them.

"Merry Christmas, my sweet girl."

Momma answers, and Dad is right there. I hear him tussling to get her phone.

"Hello, my baby. Daddy sure does miss you."

"Hi, Dad, why don't you put me on speaker so I can speak with you and mom?" He does what I ask of him. "Merry Christmas. How are you both doing?"

"We're doing good. You aren't calling to tell us you're staying in New York City, are you?"

"Dad, no questions?"

"Well, I know you are so beautiful, and when you sent us the picture of you last night, I said, 'If my girl doesn't get a husband tonight, she may not want one.'"

"Dad, you are a mess."

"Girl, I know my baby was the prettiest woman in the place."

"Daiya, that dress! Girl, it has your Momma written all over it."

"Momma, you know I'm five sizes larger than you. What in the world are you going to do with my dress?"

"Girl, I always told you, 'You can take clothes down, but you can't add to them.'"

"But you can't add to them." I recited with her mother.

"It's yours, but you did see the back, right?"

"I did, and I'll have to sew some chiffon to cover my back."

Daniel interrupted them. "When are you coming home?"

"I had plans to stay until after New Years'. I'm not sure, Dad."

"Well, enjoy yourself. I miss you, but I also know you needed this trip. Maybe, the Lord will be so gracious and give you a husband."

"Daddy, you sure keep talking about me getting a husband. "

"It might be in the atmosphere. And hey, your mother and I are not getting any younger, Daiya. If you plan on me doing PawPaw duties, you'd better get moving."

CHAPTER 23

E verything is ready, and I'm about to get my Daiya. I sit the two pitchers of orange juice and ice water on the table and step back to look at my Christmas breakfast spread. It's beautiful, and I'm proud of myself.

I turn to go towards the stairs, and I hear Daiya talking. When I focus in, and not that I'm eavesdropping, I realize she's talking to her parents. Respecting her privacy, I go back into the kitchen to take my cinnamon rolls out of the oven. I hear a noise, and I smile, thinking about Daiya's reaction to my cooking. I turn the corner to see her beautiful face and find myself staring into the eyes of Kate's parents.

What the heck are you doing here? Unannounced. No call, text, or nothing.

I'm sort of pissed, but I'm too happy to throw them out as they did me when Kate first brought me home to them. I won't be so closed-minded, and neither will I be cold. They were still a considerable part of the plan of getting Kate into the earth realm.

"Hello," I extend my hand to shack her father's hand and

hug her mother whiles speaking their names, "Kurt and Bonnie."

"We thought you'd need a little company since this is your first Christmas without our Kate." She put emphasis on *our Kate*.

"Uhm," my only response. This mess got them abandoned, but she was God's Kate now. Four years of not speaking to them because they couldn't accept me showed them who Kate belonged to, but I'm glad I played a part in their reconciliation.

When I think of them, I often think of the two thieves on the cross beside Jesus. Both were in as bad of a predicament as Jesus, but only one got the revelation of who Jesus was. The other stayed closed-minded and caught in his situation, without even the slightest consideration of what God was doing.

Kate's parents. They never got the revelation as much as I needed Kate, she needed me, and together we got the revelation of who Christ is. The reason why she now rests with Jesus, and I move forward in and with love as my guide.

You have fallen in love with Daiya, Pierce.

Right here, staring into the face of my past, I realize I love my future. "I'm not alone. God has been good to me, and things are moving along rather fine."

"By the sounds of it, Babe, I'd think he's gotten married again."

"Kurt, no. Not this soon."

"Well, he's right before you. If you care to know anything about an almost fifty-year-old man, my greatest advice would be, ask him."

"Have you gotten married?" Bonnie asked.

"Not yet," I answer. And it's incredible the only people I even thought twice about not sharing my Daiya news with are standing in my house. Lord, you sure do move in mysterious ways.

"Have a seat, and we will be down when I'm finished dressing."

"We," Bonnie exclaimed.

"Yes, you heard me, and if you have any reservations, I suggest you leave now."

"Well, you can't put us out of our daughter's house," Kurt announced.

"Your daughter's remains are closer to you than I am. So I suggest if you think you want to run anything, you go to Austin Memorial and do whatever you like."

"Why…?" Bonnie stammered, but Pierce cut her off.

"Why what? I can see it now. This visit wasn't about seeing me. There's more to why you came, so spit it out." I looked from Kurt to Bonnie. I want to say, 'piss me off if you want to,' but they both know I hold the keys. I turn to see Chuck standing in the doorway. He's ready to put them on the curb because he's never liked, Bonnie.

I nod, assuring him I'm fine. And when I'm about the hit the stairs, I see my Daiya. My entire resolve softens.

"Good morning, my love." I eagerly go towards her to whisper who's here so she won't be slighted.

Right before my very eyes, she drops the girl in the hood and goes scholar on me.

"Good morning, and who might I ask, are these fine people before us?"

My eyes buck, but only she and Chuck can see me. He giggles softly, and I kiss her gently on the lips. "These are the parents of,"

"Kate?" She answers me.

"Yes, sweetheart," I answer, and she moves around me.

"Good morning, Mr. and Mrs. Hollingsworth. It is a pleasure to meet the people who birth such a beautiful soul into the earth."

"Good mooor," Kurt stumbled.

"Morning Dear," Bonnie acts as though she was more concerned about pulling the word out of Kurt.

It wasn't a surprise. Kurt was mesmerized. Daiya looked like an angel if angels are as beautiful as we expect them to be.

With such finesse and charm, she grabs Bonnie's hand and escorts her to the sofa.

"Kate is such a dear soul, and I know she's smiling down from heaven at the gathering of her loved ones."

"She was so precious," Bonnie answered Daiya.

"She was, and her blessings over Pierce and I has given me all I've needed to love him for the rest of our lives."

"Yes," Bonnie answers as if she knows what the heck Daiya is saying.

"And you, Mr. Kurt, it is, right?"

"Ye, ye, ye Yes," he stuttered, causing Chuck to roll back into the dining room laughing in silence.

"You are more handsome in person than you are on any of these photos. I bet you're hungry." Daiya winked at him.

He blushed but never answered her.

"Well, why don't you and Bonnie help us enjoy this feast baby has made for us. He's such a wonderful man, and I know he poured his heart in this breakfast."

She guided them to the dining room as if she were the lady of the house. Kurt was smiling so hard when Daiya grabbed his hands, and Bonnie, enthralled by her, kept looking at me to see my expression.

My face remained stoic the entire time.

They both had one time to offend Daiya, and it was a wrap. I was throwing them out so fast they'd remember how they did me. But, thanks to Daiya, they made it this time.

By the time breakfast was over, she and Kurt were so deep into a conversation about gumbo and jambalaya until Bonnie and I were left to talk to one another. I led Bonnie back into the living room and told her I'd be back.

Chuck stopped me in the hallway. "Boss, Daiya is something else. She knew they were prejudice, but she didn't even give their thoughts time to fester. Daiya is worth the diamond and position as Mrs. Jansen."

"Man, she did a number on them, didn't she?"

"She sure did, and I'm so impressed I almost got jealous and told Kurt to find him a black beauty and get out of Daiya's face." We laugh so hard because we both knew Kurt couldn't cook a lick.

By the time everyone was seated in the family room, I wanted to find out the real reason they had come to New York.

"Kurt, Bonnie, what's going on?

"Bonnie looked at Daiya."

"It's okay, Bonnie. Daiya is a part of me, and if you want me to continue as a part of your family, Daiya comes with me."

"I understand. Kurt, tell Pierce what we need."

"Pierce, I've run into some financial troubles. Things are hard, and I needed a little help."

"Enough said."

"What do you mean?"

"Kurt, Kate, and I have succored your future. Chuck, bring my bag."

Chuck brought my bag. I looked at Daiya, and she nodded and smiled. I knew it was the right thing to do. I handed Kurt and Bonnie a check for seven million dollars.

"Pierce, is this right?"

"We didn't need this much. We only needed a couple of thousand." Bonnie shook her head as if she were taking something from me. I couldn't afford to give.

"Bonnie, it's yours. Kate and I decided we didn't want you all to worry about anything. I knew Kate always helped you guys. As I have with my parents, and this is not a loan or a hand-out, Kurt."

Kurt nodded as he wiped away tears.

"You have been a stellar businessman, but even the best of them sometimes fall on hard times. But here's something Kate taught me. As long as you keep investing in the Kingdom, you'll never be broke. God will have men to give in to your bosom. So, look at this as God giving you back all the seeds you have sown."

I look at Daiya, and without even having to ask her, I know she believes in the principle of tithing and the manifestation of seed, sowing, and harvesting.

Kurt shook his head as he held Bonnie's hand, "We have sown plenty seeds, and by the look of this check, it's been in good ground."

"And part of your good ground was Kate and me. You deserve to live the rest of your lives without a care in the world, but caring for others like you do."

"Thank you, son."

CHAPTER 24

When Pierce told me about Kate's will, I knew regardless of how her parents treated him, the right thing to do was give them the best Christmas gift they have ever had. Sure, it wouldn't bring their daughter back, but it would help them to endure the pain of losing her.

My Daddy says, 'Money helps those who are grieving focus their attention on something other than the lost.'

I believe him. I've seen the difference firsthand with the parishioners. If they received a lump sum of money after a loved one's death, they would reconstruct their lives. The memories become the cornerstone for their new foundation. But I've also seen the wombs of those who have to shake a can to bury their loved ones and fall into deeper debt after they die. It becomes like punishment on top of pain.

I watched Pierce intensely. He was still having trouble with his decision to release what was theirs. Not because he needed it, but because of the clause. I'd never judge him because I know how hard it is to bless people who hurt you. But, I also know God honors integrity. He also told us to bless those who despitefully misuse us. So there it is, Pierce's opportunity to bless the people who were once his enemy.

I can relate.

At my job, I deal with a lot of people; some prejudiced, some not. I've learned no matter how you treat me—if I treat you as though you are a child of the Most High God—you'll see me in the light of Christ, even if it takes you a while.

I could see a look in Bonnie's eyes I've seen over and over again. But I could also see when the devil of division's neck got cut. Bonnie's eyes soften, right when her heart opened.

And after Pierce blessed them with their check, Bonnie and Kurt cried and thanked the Lord. One thing I realize, we all go through tough times, and sometimes the very one you hate or dislike is the very one who may hold your blessing in their hands.

If I didn't know any better, I'd say the Lord allowed the most significant test to be before them. First, they needed to humble themselves to ask for help. Then, they had to restrain themselves when they walked into something they disagreed with or didn't like. The hardest thing in the world for some people. Humility and restraint.

I walked over to the grand piano, pull the stool out, and sat down, and I began to play.

Pierce's eyes got so huge. He doesn't know everything about me, how could he? Sooner or later, he'll learn as much as he was praying for me, my Daddy and Mother has been praying for him.

Pierce unhooked the guitar from the wall and began following me. Even Chuck came back into the room. I winked at him and smiled because I could see so much in his facial expression.

"I wanted to praise a little to help you, Bonnie and Kurt, praise God for all He's doing. May I?" I pointed to the piano, and everyone nodded.

But Bonnie said, "Hallelujah!"

"Baby, follow me. I wrote this little song about three years ago." I blew Pierce a kiss because he was surprised.

♪♪"Memories of You, being born in a manger.

Memories of You, wrapped in swaddling clothes.

Memories of You, the Wisemen came to see;

That Christ is born.

I wasn't there, but I've always been told.

And these are the things I dearly hold.

Sweet memories, I'll share, even when I'm old.

It's sweet memories, in my heart, that warms my soul.

It's sweet memories, in my heart, that warms my soul.

Memories of You, who grew into a man.

Memories of You, teaching those who'd understand.

Memories of You, the One they crucified;

On Calvary.

I wasn't there, but I've always been told.

And these are the things I dearly hold.

Sweet memories, I'll share, even when I'm old.

It's sweet memories, in my heart, that warms my soul.

You have allowed me to know Your warm embrace.

You have allowed me to feel amazing grace.

You have allowed me to feel the love You give.

Some things were just from memory,

But now You're real to me.

Now, I pass on all the memories, all the memories I have when You were born, and when You died, and then You chose Me to live inside.

I'll forever hold the memories.

I'll forever hold all of the memories.

I'll forever hold the memories.

In my heart and soul."♪♪

"Daiya," Pierce called my name and then joined me on the piano.

"You wrote that?"

"I did. Bonnie, don't cry." I said, feeling like I song to cheer them, not make her sad.

Bonnie blew her nose with the Kleenex Chuck handed her. After Kurt held her and allowed her to cry, she told me she knew Kate had a conversation with God concerning me. By the time she finished, we all were crying. I think we were all praising the Lord and thinking of the memories we had of Him, moving, blessing, and even in the taking of Kate.

"We hold them forever in our hearts, and we are all grateful. Not only for the life of Christ, but for the lasting memories, He gives each of us of His grace, mercy, kindness, long-suffering, and most of all, of His love." Pierce said.

I began to play Away In A Manger, which led to Silent Night and Jingle Bells. By the time we finished playing, singing and laughing, it was after two o'clock. Kurt and Bonnie announced they were staying at The Wellington until after New Years'.

Pierce told him staying there wasn't necessary, and they should go and get their things and come back to where Kate would want them to be. I agreed. And then it hit me. Pierce should keep the house as a vacation spot for them and Kate's siblings. They could use it as an Air BnB.

We bid farewell to Kurt and Bonnie, and although it could have been horrible, God made it one of the best Christmas' of our lives.

When we waved at them pulling out the driveway, Pierce pulled me into his arms and kissed me as though he had been waiting on this all day. The more he held me, the more he solidified our connection.

He pulled his lips away and stared into my eyes, "Little lady, you promised to marry me today, but I have somewhere to take you."

"You do?"

"Yes. You can go upstairs, put on your coat, boots, and pack your things or you can go upstairs, put on your coat, boats, and pack your things."

"What great choices, Pierce?" We both laughed.

I didn't have a clue where Pierce was taking me. I tried to get it out of Chuck, but he was as tight-lipped as Pierce. I looked at my clothes. Lord, please don't let this man be taking me to get married looking like this.

We made it to The Wellington, and I figured we'd be getting married in the ballroom, but Pierce had my bags packed and waiting on us downstairs. I looked at him, now feeling perturbed because someone has been all up in my panty business.

I'm going to get used to Pierce reading my mind, now or never. He looked at me as soon as I turned at the sight of my luggage.

"My trusted assistant had his wife to pack your bags for me. I trust her with your underwear." He laughed.

"How did you know I was a little put-off?"

"Daiya, we've been talking for days, and I know when you feel some sort of way. I also know how private you are? Most professional people are, but also holy people. And you, my dear, fall in both spaces.

We laughed. He was right. I wasn't over the top holy, but while the angels are before the throne shouting 'Holy, holy, holy,' I'm in the mix with my, 'Hallelujah.'

And, I was thinking about someone looking at my panties. Private property and I have no desire to let anyone, even Pierce, see mine until I'm paid with commitment.

I need a man to do more than put a ring on it. My song says, 'Put a ring on it and sign the papers you got from the court-house.' Period.

"Okay, so, you still haven't told me where I'm going. Does Quanie know about this? Who else knows besides Chuck?"

"Listen, do you believe I have you?"

"I know you do."

"Do you believe I'll never hurt you?"

"I know you'll never hurt me."

"Do you trust me, Daiya?"

I think for a while. The question could make or break me, so I search my heart. I wanted it to be a heart matter instead of a head matter, so I reasoned with myself, asking the question from a philosophical stance. Can you trust a man you've only known for a little while? Then I make the most astonishing, most profound statement. "I trust you, Pierce, because I trust God's in you."

He grabs, hugs, and kisses me. And in my Bible talk, I say, "I have answered correctly."

CHAPTER 25

A

ll I needed was to know was she trusts me. Now I know, I'm never looking back. I've already set the tone for this next move because I didn't want nor need any surprises.

From all of the information I gathered, Daniel Pierce was a force to reckon with.

I went into my marriage to Kate with disgruntled parents who felt as though we blocked them from the moment they'd waited for all of her life. I couldn't do an injustice to the Prince family. This time, I was doing this marriage thing the right way from the beginning until death brought it to an end.

Chuck and Deacon are taking Daiya to the car while I handle an urgent matter. But, knowing Daiya, if I stay too long, she'll come looking for me. I'm trying to make sure when we go back to New York, The Wellington will host our wedding banquet.

I smile as my mind drifts back to the call I made early this morning.

"Mr. Prince," I ask.

"Yes, this is he." I can hear the hesitation in his voice.

"I'm Pierce Jansen. You do not know me, but I've come to know and love your daughter."

"Okay." He answers, but I hear hesitation.

"I've asked Daiya to marry me, but I would like to have your permission."

"Son, if Daiya loves you, we'll love you. My daughter is an excellent judge of character, and believe me when I say, Daiya does nothing except what she wants to do."

"I understand. And yes, Daiya's very head-strong. But there's more. I'm white, and I'm forty-six." I wait for him to say something, but he laughs.

"I'm black, and I'm seventy." He belts out.

We both laugh, and I hear her mother in the background, and then he places me on speaker.

"Baby, this is Pierce, and he wants to marry our girl. I told you, any man would be a fool to let our beauty leave New York the way she came."

"Well, Sir, I'm not the fool, and although she'll be coming back like she came, it won't be for long. But I do need help. You deserve to walk your daughter down the aisle, so would you by chance have a friend who could marry us?"

"Man, I'm a pastor. I have thirty right here who I can ask, but only one I'd trust my daughter's vows with; me. So I'll walk her and then get in my position."

"Perfect, you have no arguments from me."

"And Mother Alma, Daiya, trust your judgment on everything. Can I send you some money and you make sure my bride has the most beautiful gown around. Also, can you hire First Lady Destiny Strong on short notice?"

"I surely can. I'm Destiny's mentor, and we'll have everything ready. Now tell me this, can we do it tomorrow instead of on Christmas Day and make it a night wedding?"

"Yes. I can wait one more day, but I can't promise you two."

"All I'll need is a day to get the word out to our family and close

friends. Knowing Daiya, she'll want Quanie as her maid of honor."

"Yes, ma'am, and I believe someone will be knocking at your door in 5, 4, 3, 2, 1." And as I said, the currier started knocking.

He asked if Mr. Prince could sign for the package, and as he took the package, Pierce began to explain.

"There's one-hundred—thousand-dollars in the envelope."

Alma gasped, and Daniel chuckled at his wife.

I continued, "If you can get as much as you can to give Daiya the wedding of her dream, I'd appreciate it, and anything you have to spend above that, I will give it back to you when we arrive."

"Deal. But aren't the parents of the bride supposed to pay for the wedding?" Daniel asked.

"Mr. Prince used the money you've saved for Daiya's wedding as a gift for you and Mrs. Alma for bringing my rib into the earth. I know the Lord has used you countless times, but I promise, whereas it concerns Daiya Treshelle Prince, it was all for me."

"Let the church say, 'Amen.' And we will be good stewards over your money, Son."

"I know you will, and please, spare nothing. Mrs. Alma, I want it to be a day she'll never forget."

"Between you and us, Daiya's has a wedding board she's worked on for years. I know where to get everything she desires. She didn't understand why she kept it up, but I often encouraged her to add to it. Well, to be honest, she's made this easy for us. So, you men folks, let me go so I can get started. And if you don't mind, I'll feel safer writing checks and then letting Pastor put the money back in the bank."

"Whatever you do is fine with me. I'm not expecting any change back and again, if you use any of your own money, I will give it to you when we arrive."

"Boy, what? You made of money? I always knew my baby girl was worthy of a prince, but are you?"

"Am I what? A prince?"

"Yeah. Throwing around all this money like it was leaves."

"No, Sir, I'm a man who loves God, one who tithes, and one who

has made the Kingdom my first investment. God continues to bless me, and I will be insane not to use my blessing to make the most special woman in the world happy on her wedding day."

"Well, praise Jesus. My baby girl dune found her a man of God."

"No, Sir, I'm not a preacher."

Daniel Prince laughed so hard. "Son, you don't have to be a preacher to be a man of God. You have to be a man after God's own heart."

"I am. Thank you. I'd better get moving because I need to get Daiya fed and back to Louisiana today."

I paid for the ballroom and spoke with Carson for a minute. Things were changing, but I refused to allow the temperature of love to come down one degree. After things were in order, I made my way to the SUV, where Daiya waited for me.

As soon as I opened the door, she complained, "It's been long enough."

I climbed in and gently turned her face back towards me. "Are you mad at me for the first time?"

"I am," she rolled her eyes, causing me to laugh. I turned her face back to me again and captured her mouth in a long kiss.

"Pierce, you have to stop kissing me every time as if we'd said, 'I do.'"

"Girl, every time I kiss you is an I Do moment. I do, love you. I do, want you. I do, need you in my life. And I do want you to be my wife."

"You are so full of it, Pierce, but I do too."

"Okay, since we have your mad moment out of the way. We are going on a trip. Are you ready?"

"Pierce to where?"

"It's a secret, but I'm taking you away to marry you. You good with it?"

"You are so full of surprises. Yes, but I would've liked to tell Quanie I'm leaving."

"She'll be alright. For the first time in your lives since college, you both will be making a decision for yourselves."

"Really, Pierce, are you jealous?"

"No, but I will take first place, and she'll move to second. Right?"

"No, Sir. My relationship with you can't be put in a place-ment system. I am you. Quanie will still be first like Carson, Chuck, and Brad will still be whatever number they fall in with you."

"Yes, ma'am. No, technically, since we have about ten minutes before we get to the hanger, we can kiss the entire time, or you can tell me something else you think I should know about my future wife."

"I've told you everything."

"Are you sure?"

"Well, I'm mean when I'm hungry. I love food, so I workout five times a week so I won't get another size bigger. I love being a size sixteen, and I'm the happiest woman in the world because of you."

"See, I was trying not to kiss you, but you're making it hard for me."

After acting like two teenagers kissing before they make it home after a date, we get to the hanger. Then, Chuck takes our bags, and I walk Daiya to my airplane. No, our plane. I'm going to have to get used to saying our instead of my all the time. Daiya climbs the stairs and is blown away when she sees Jansen written on the seats."Pierce, a plane?"

"Girl, why do you think I'd let my wife continue to teach in Louisiana if I didn't have provisions to get to her whenever I'd like. I might look crazy, but I'm not."

Daiya threw her head back and laughed so hard Chuck and I couldn't help but join in. We waited for a while, and when Brad and his wife Emily arrived, we left New York. I intro-duced them both to my Daiya and explained it was Emily who packed her things. By the time we landed, they were friends. They talked about everything from the video left by Kate to living as a P. K. Emily, fully engulfed in Daiya's every word, had been entertained. And Daiya can be so funny. She had us all laughing.

But when we got off the plane, and Daiya realized we were in Shreveport, she immediately began to cry.

"Come on now, Daiya, you're making everyone cry." I pleaded, but nothing worked.

CHAPTER 26

Not only was I at home for Christmas, but I had the love of my life and his closest friends at home with me. I only wished Quanie and Carson could be here with us. Emily was sweet, and all but no one could take the place of Quanie.

Pierce had an SUV waiting for us. After we all got in, I knew we were going to my house. Little did I know, Pierce Jansen knew where he was going, and he didn't need my help.

When we pulled into my parent's circular drive, we all got out of the car. It wasn't long before my parents were out of the house and hugging both Pierce and me like they already knew him.

He introduced them to his friends, and I watched, stunned as can be.

"Okay, wait a minute. Pierce, you already know my parents?"

"Baby, I had to ask your Dad for your hand in marriage. How rude do you think I am?"

I threw my arms around him and hugged him as if I was

hugging Santa himself. And like he'd done for the last few days, Pierce made me cry.

"Come on, Daddy's big baby," my Dad pulled me into his arms. "Didn't I tell you a man would be a fool to let you leave there and not stake a claim? Well, Pierce did, and I'm so proud of you. You did good, baby girl. He loves the Lord and you."

I cried harder.

Not only has this man been in contact with my parents. He asked them to marry me and brought me home to them. What a wonderful Christmas this is turning out to be? I only wished Quanie were here.

"Well, why are you still crying, Daiya?"

"How will I get married without Quanie. Momma, Quanie's not here." I whaled.

"Baby, I know you want your sister here, but sometimes you have to be a big girl apart from her."

"But Momma," I whined.

"I know, Daiya, and if I could do anything to get her here, I would, baby. I'm so sorry. But hey, why don't we enjoy tonight and allow tomorrow to take care of itself."

"Okay, Mom, and she and Emily hug me."

Mom gives everyone instructions.

"Go put your bags up and wash up. It's time to eat our Christmas dinner."

All you could hear were hungry men eagerly saying, "Yes, ma'am."

Emily and I disappear into the kitchen to help Momma. The table is spread, and Daniel and Alma's feast is getting ready to go down.

I move around getting utensils and setting plates out because my parents don't believe in paper anything—old school to the heart. The vast dining room table we've never used is worth the money Mom paid for it. Seven of the chairs have only been sat in once or twice.

It's incredible how most pastors have tons of children, but my parents only have Quanie and me.

I'm shocked how Emily, a white girl, moves around this kitchen like she knows how to work. Girlfriend washing and rinsing dishes, and she's even rinsing out glasses and filling them with ice.

"You go, Emily," I said from across the room.

"Daiya, I come from pentecostal parents, and there are ten of us. One thing I know is how to respect a kitchen and the cook."

"Girl, I couldn't imagine having nine siblings."

"It's mass production. Everything. Especially Christmas. I'm missing them this year, but I do every other year with them. Brad is an only child like yourself, so his brothers are Pierce, Chuck, and Carson. I'm glad I'll have another girl in our bunch. All we have to do now is find Chuck, a wife."

"You two stay out of his business and allow the Lord to handle His good business. Now, put those napkins on the side of their plates, and I'll go get Dad and the men."

Emily and I both answer, 'Yes ma'am,' but I'm already trying to see which one of my cousins can do a pop-up.

Emily looks at me, and she laughs, and then I laugh. "You're trying to figure out who to call for, Chuck, aren't you."

"Emily, what? You read my face too."

"Girl, Pierce warned me. He said you could not hide anything because if you feel it, it will show on your face."

"I think he's right. I'm going to practice because I cannot spend the rest of my life with a man who knows my every thought. It'll be like the movie "What Men Want.""

"I know, right. All I can say is it could be bad but also good. At least Pierce won't have to guess."

"Guess about what?" Pierce asked, coming around the corner.

"Oh, you. Stop being nosey already. We're not even married, and you're acting like my Daddy."

"How is he acting like your Daddy?"

"Busted," Pierce yells, and I look like a deer in headlights.

"Keep on Pierce Jansen."

"And you'll do what." He asks, looking smug as if I won't say what I want to in front of my Daddy.

"You better recognize. Daniel Prince is Daddy first, and then the pastor. So, he cannot save you in Daddy mode."

"Okay. Okay. I'm waving the white flag for sure." He comes over and kisses me, and then he sits down by my Daddy.

When everyone is seated, Daddy clears his throat, and we all get quiet.

"I am honored to have each of you as our special guest for this special occasion. God does work in mysterious ways. To be honest, I didn't want my baby going to New York for Christmas, but God told me to be quiet. I closed my mouth and obeyed. Now, look at this table. If my baby hadn't gone, none of you would be here. I know He's the God of multiplication, and I'm honored to call Him Master and King."

"Amen," flowed around the table.

"Let us pray. Father, You do all things well. We thank You for these, Your children, who sit at the table. We pray You will bless us individually but collectively. Bless the two who are ready to add You to the equation of marriage. For we believe a three-stranded-cord can never break. Now, bless the food. The hands which have prepared it. Lord cause it to be nourishment for our bodies, taking our any infirmities, but allowing it to heal our bodies. We thank You for food, family, fellowship, and most of all, for Your Son, Jesus. In Jesus' name, we pray. Amen."

"Amen," chimed around the table again.

"Oh Lord, please bless the cook and give her the strength to cook for me looking as pretty as she did the first day I married her, as long as I live."

Everyone laughed.

"Oh, Daniel, fix your plate, man." Momma blushed.

I watched Pierce, watching the banter between them. He laughed, and I could see nothing but joy in his eyes. I'm so happy, but at the same time, I'm feeling the missing pieces of me.

It's crazy to be alone all of your life, and then God brings a friend who sticks closer than a brother. My Quanie. She means the world to me, and I expect her at my big moments. But, I have to get used to things as they are. I'm moving to New York, and we'll still be so far away."

CHAPTER 27

Dinner was everything. I was so in awe of the way my Daiya acts around her parents. I see another side of her, and I love it. She's treating them how she treated Kate's parents, so now I know it was Daiya. No show. No faking. Pure love and affection for those in her presence.

When I awakened this morning, Mr. Prince was already at the kitchen table drinking coffee. I joined him. We talked about everything from church to work. Then he shared with me the name of one of the pastors in New York.

The craziest thing is my construction company built the same pastor's church. Daniel Prince was shocked and glad. I chuckled, remembering what he said.

"You are a blessing for my daughter and The Christian Love Assembly. Man, I need a new church and look at God. Done sent me a whole builder in my family."

I could see precisely where Daiya gets her upfront in-your-face attitude from. He wasn't concerned or ashamed to tell me exactly what he wanted and needed. And to be honest, it's the very thing I promised to spend my portion of Kate's will on. I will be helping people who need help.

When I told him I'll be living back and forwards but mainly in Louisiana until Daiya finished her school year, he praised the Lord. So, I already know Mr. Prince has my work cut out for me.

I excused myself when I noticed Carson calling me back.

"Hey, man, how's everything going?"

"It's fine. How are you and Daiya?"

"Man, we're good. We are in Louisiana, and I'm planning a surprise wedding today. Do you think you can get Quanie here? Man, she's happy, miserable. She won't be happy as she could be without Quanie."

"Man, I understand. Those two are like sisters."

"Yes, and I surely don't want my wife disappointed on our special day."

"Well, what time is the wedding?"

"It's a night wedding, so I think it's starting at seven o'clock. And another thing, will you be my best man?"

"I thought you'd never ask. Heck yeah."

"Okay, I'll have you a suit and Quanie's dress waiting for you. You can change at the venue when you arrive."

"Perfect. So, I need to get a move on it."

"I pray safe travels for the two of you, and we'll see you when you get here."

I hung up the phone and went back into the kitchen.

"Looks like Quanie's going to make it, but I'll let it be a surprise for Daiya."

"Praise the Lord. I've been praying about that all night. Much as I have to pray for Quanie's mouth, I'd still rather she be right where we are than not here."

"I understand. Quanie can be a sailor when she wants to be. But you've done something right."

"What?" Pastor Daniel asks.

"The most I've ever heard Daiya say was 'hell.' And she was ashamed."

"She's a good girl. I'm not lying, but so is Quanie. I believe old habits die hard."

"You've said a mouthful."

"Okay, so what's the plan," I ask.

"Mother and I have everything set. All you have to do is show up at the church's men's quarters. There are dressing rooms and everything you need in there like drinks, snacks, and a television. Mother will have Emily and Daiya at the beauty and nail shop. Mother asked Emily and one of Daiya's cousins, Mariah, to be a bride's maid. So, everyone except Daiya knows what's going on."

Mother whisk Emily and me to the Mall as soon as it opened. We shopped until I was too tired to do anything. But mom insisted we go to the beauty salon, and she's paying for our hair and nails. What a wonderful treat? My hair needed shampoo and to get back to my curls. I thought about getting it flat ironed, but Momma persuaded me to keep it natural and get a bun.

The stylist made it so pretty, and I knew today was my day —the day after Christmas. A wedding. How extraordinary will our lives be? I looked at myself again and again, and I had to admit, I was beautiful.

We did lunch at Superior Steakhouse, and the food was delicious. I could have gone to the house and got in bed, but Mom insisted on keeping me moving. And, by the time we made it back to the house, all the men were gone.

I took a bath, being careful not to mess my hair up. And once I finished, I went to lay down across my bed. Somewhere between thankful and tired, I fell into a deep sleep. By the time I woke up, there was a wedding dress hanging on my door.

"Mother," I yelled.

"Yes," she, Emily, and my cousin Mariah turned the corner together.

They all had their faces beat. Emily and Mariah wore the blush pink one-shoulder gowns I chose for my bride's maids.

"Mom, is today the day?"

"Yes, it is, Daiya."

"Oh, Mom, but how did you find the dresses?"

"I had Jourdain's to make me a dress for the girls and of course you."

"Oh, Mom," I threw my arms around her neck.

"Now, don't start crying, and come on so we can dress you."

I grab my phone and call Quanie, but I get no answer.

"Daiya put the phone down and come on here so we can get you in this dress. The SUV will be here to pick us up in thirty minutes."

"Yes, ma'am." I place the phone back on my dresser. I look up at a picture of Quanie and me on my wall. I nearly get choked. She gives me something different for Christmas, and now she's too grown to be by my side.

I surely don't like the trade-off, but I pray everything is going better for her and Carson.

Momma pulls the dress out of the bag, and I cry. She's got my dress. The dress I've dreamt of being married in. It's an off the shoulder long sleeves mermaid dress with crystals all over the front and a deep V in the back. A J. Jourdain special, and it fits me like a glove.

I turn to Momma, and now she and Emily both are crying. I try to keep my composure because my head is already hurting. We gather anything Momma thinks I might need and go out to get in the SUV.

I'm nervous and trembling.

Emily catches my hands. "Father, we thank you for this new love. Allow peace to flow over Daiya and take every care and concern into Your hands, in Jesus' name. Amen."

"Amen," Momma, Mariah, and I said. I closed my eyes because, in addition to Quanie, God has blessed me with another sister and a cousin who is special. I have to be grateful and content.

When we arrive at the church, the outside decorations are beautiful. I look over at Momma, and she hunches her shoulders. She's been rambling, and I'm so thankful. The outside of Dad's church looked how I envisioned; white lights and artificial snow—a winter wonderland wedding.

"No tears. No tears," I remind myself.

We get out of the vehicle. We quickly make our way through the doubled doors and around to the lady's quarters. Momma opens the door, and I walk in behind her.

"It's about time you made it," I hear, and I stand still and start shaking my head.

Then Quanie whispers in my ear, "Girl, don't make me call you out of your name in the Lord's house."

I start squealing, and she's as loud as I am. I knew Quanie wouldn't let me down. I knew my sister wouldn't miss the most special day of my life.

Momma is crying as hard as we are. And I look around to see Emily and Mariah both crying.

Quanie leaned in, dabbing tears from her eyes, and whispered in my ear. "This is why I can't fu... Uh, mess with you." We snicker. "I was beat, and now we look like clowns. Who's going to fix my makeup?" Quanie stops talking and looks at me. "Love looks good on you, Daiya."

"I hugged her and said, 'I knew you'd be here. I knew my sister was coming. I knew it.'"

To be honest, I didn't, but I sure wanted her to be right by my side. Momma tells us to hurry up because she was getting ready to walk in, and we'd have to get everyone in place. But, First Lady Destiny Strong stood in the gap. She jumped right in, helping us to restore our make-up and keep us in order. My bride's maid walked down the aisle, leaving Quanie and me alone.

"This is some Christmas," Quanie says and grabs my hand. "We went to New York to get away and look at us."

"Look at God."

"Look at Him and look at you." Quanie's eyes fill with tears, and so does mine. "PawPaw wasn't playing. Got us all decked out. Carson flew me in on a private plane. Is this my life? Because I can't stop crying."

We went to New York, got found by two billionaires, and having a Christmas wedding. But I'm so glad he didn't have me waiting on my kiss like in the Hallmark movies.

"Me either. Someone tell my tears to come back tomorrow." We laugh.

"You dared to do something different, and now you're starting a new life."

"Won't He do it!" We say in unison.

"Won't He do it? Change your life and situation, like that," she popped her fingers. "Quanie, I'm so in love. I can't imagine my life without Pierce. I'm so glad that I still trust you and those crazy games you play. Thinking back on that night, I was so upset that of all the men in that lounge, you picked PawPaw. But PawPaw is what the Doctor ordered. And believe me, I'm talking about Doctor Jesus."

"Imma leave that one to you. I already prayed today. I'm tapped out on my Bible knowledge."

I shake my head because I know God's gonna save Quanie yet. "I love you, Sissy," I tell her, and this time I dabbed her tears away. "Momma said, you're next, and I believe her. So, get ready, and I better be standing right next to you like you'll be standing right next to me. And Quanie, don't make me laugh."

"I won't, but I can't make any promises if Momma Alma starts that shouting. Remember when she kicked off her shoes and hit someone in the front row. Girl, if she does *that*, I got jokes for days."

Quanie kisses Daddy, and he tries to lay hands on her, but she swats him off as usual. He knows he loves her almost as much as he loves me.

Daddy laughs, "I can't wait until the Holy Spirit catches her. I pray I'm there to witness it."

"Me too." I giggle. "Daddy, and you almost made me miss all of this."

"Girl, you are like me If I had tried to push you to marry anyone else, you would have torn this town to pieces."

"I guess I am Daniel Prince's daughter."

"That you are."

Then I heard our song, My Song by H. E. R. Daddy smiles.

"You ready, baby girl?" Daddy asks.

"I'm ready," I smile, and the doors open, and the only person I see is Pierce Jansen. My something different for Christmas.

EPILOGUE

My baby and I are married now. The wedding was more than I'd ever expected. When I tell you, my Momma had everything exactly the way I wanted it. And by the time I made it down to my Pierce, everyone was crying.

Including Daddy, who doesn't allow secular music to play in the church, but he said it was such a beautiful love song, he couldn't deny Pierce.

And to make it even more memorable, Pierce had the artist come to our wedding and sing her song. I could've...I can't even explain it.

Daddy finally got himself together to officiate our wedding vows, but he was emotional the entire wedding. Rightly so. I am his only baby girl. Well, biological girl, because as much as he and Quanie's love-hate relationship plays out in public, everyone knows he loves her like his own.

I don't know what was more exciting, Pierce kissing me as if it were his very first time, Quanie screaming, 'Girl, you's married now,' or Pierce carrying me over the threshold of my home, now—our home.

There are red roses from my front door to my bedroom. He's got wine, chilled glasses, strawberries, and even finger foods.

I love this man. He knows what his baby needs. I promise I was too busy speaking to people and dancing at the little mock reception to eat anything but the piece of cake Pierce put in my mouth for our photos.

Right before we left the reception venue, I hugged everyone. I hated to leave my girl, but I could tell she and Carson were as tired as everyone else was. I'm glad they made it, and Carson looked rather handsome standing beside my man, watching Quanie the entire time. Ask me how I know.

Momma was watching everything and said with her mouth, 'Quanie's going to be next."

Only if Carson can keep her from acting a nut, but I'm team Momma from the looks of things. They are in love, and it shows.

But before I left, I whispered to Quanie, 'I'm moving to New York,' and guess what? So is she. Hot dog! Look at God.

Sometimes, it makes me think who wouldn't serve a God like mine. And I tell people, 'Look back over your life. I promise you'll see Him in spaces you never thought He'd be.'

I surely didn't think He would have let me be found in New York, but I'm so grateful He did. And thankful I'm alive to see the best Christmas I've ever had in my life. It's only going to get better, and Pierce told me he had better be right by my side the next time I searched for something different.

Trust me. He will. And I pray I have three or four little Pierce look-alike right behind me.

Okay, I have to go because now I'm about to get something different for my wedding night. Goodnight.

Merry Christmas
The End

SPECIAL THANKS

If you enjoyed Daiya & Pierce's Story
Something Different For Christmas
by Author Danyelle Scroggins (Sweet)
Please Leave a Review &
Would you like to read Quanie & Carson's Story?
No Searching just click....
Grown and Sexy For Christmas
by Author Ja'Nese Dixon

Thank you for supporting us. We really appreciate you. Merry
Christmas & Happy New Year!

ACKNOWLEDGMENTS

I am so happy and honored to have been half of this phenomenal duo adventure. There's nothing like having a friend who sticks closer than a brother, and Dana's been that type of friend.

Thank sis, for this beautiful adventure. May God continue to bless you and your family.

Your bonus sister,

Danyelle

ABOUT THE AUTHOR

Danyelle Scroggins is the Pastor of New Vessels Ministries in Shreveport, Louisiana. She is the author of special books like Put It In Ink, Graced After The Pain, Evonta's Revenge, & Enduring Love. Danyelle is wife of Pastor Reynard Scroggins and the mother of three young adults: Raiyawna, Dobrielle, and Dwight Jr. by birth; and two: Reynard II and Gabriel by marriage. The privilege of being a mother graciously presented her with the impressive task of now being the grandmother of Emiya'rai Grace, RC III, & Maddox Rai.

Danyelle loves writing inspirational stories set in Louisiana, where she lives preaching, teaching, and enjoying writing by the window. Learn all about her here www. danyellescroggins.com.

For exclusives Join My Mailing List!

Also find her on Facebook, Twitter, and Bookbub.

If you liked this book, please take a few minutes to leave a review now! Authors appreciate this as it is helpful in drawing more readers to books they too might enjoy. Thanks!

facebook.com/authordanyellescroggins
twitter.com/pastordanyelle
bookbub.com/profile/danyelle-scroggins
goodreads.com/danyellescroggins

OTHER BOOKS BY DANYELLE

Faith Temple Cathedral Books
Destiny's Decision
More Than Diamonds

A Louisiana Love Series
The Right Choice
The Wrong Decision
The Perfect Chance
The Blessed Opportunity

A Louisiana Christmas
Love Me Again
Never Looking Back
The Complete Set: A La. Christmas

The Power Series Rebirth
Graced After The Pain
Grace Restored
Grace Realized
Grace Revealed

E Love Series

Enduring Love
Enchanting Love
Everlasting Love
Extraordinary Love
Extravagant Love

The Power Series Rebirth

Graced After The Pain
Grace Restored
Grace Realized
Grace Revealed
The Complete Set: Graced AfterThe Pain

Stand Alone

Put It In Ink
Evonta's Revenge

Made in the USA
Columbia, SC
26 September 2024

42437759R00105